BIRTH ROAD

Michelle Wamboldt

Vagrant
PRESS

Vagrant Press is an imprint of
Nimbus Publishing Limited
3660 Strawberry Hill St, Halifax, NS, B3K 5A9
(902) 455-4286 nimbus.ca

Printed and bound in Canada

Design: Heather Bryan
Editor: Whitney Moran
NB1568

This is a work of fiction. While certain characters are inspired by persons no longer living, and certain events by events which may have happened, the story is a work of the imagination not to be taken as a literal or documentary representation of its subject.

Library and Archives Canada Cataloguing in Publication

Title: Birth road / Michelle Wamboldt.
Names: Wamboldt, Michelle, author.
Identifiers: Canadiana 20210381159 | ISBN 9781774710401 (softcover)
Classification: LCC PS8645.A4985 B57 2022 | DDC C813/.6—dc23

Nimbus Publishing acknowledges the financial support for its publishing activities from the Government of Canada, the Canada Council for the Arts, and from the Province of Nova Scotia. We are pleased to work in partnership with the Province of Nova Scotia to develop and promote our creative industries for the benefit of all Nova Scotians.

The weak can never forgive.
Forgiveness is the attribute of the strong.
—*Mahatma Gandhi*

For Mom and Old Nan

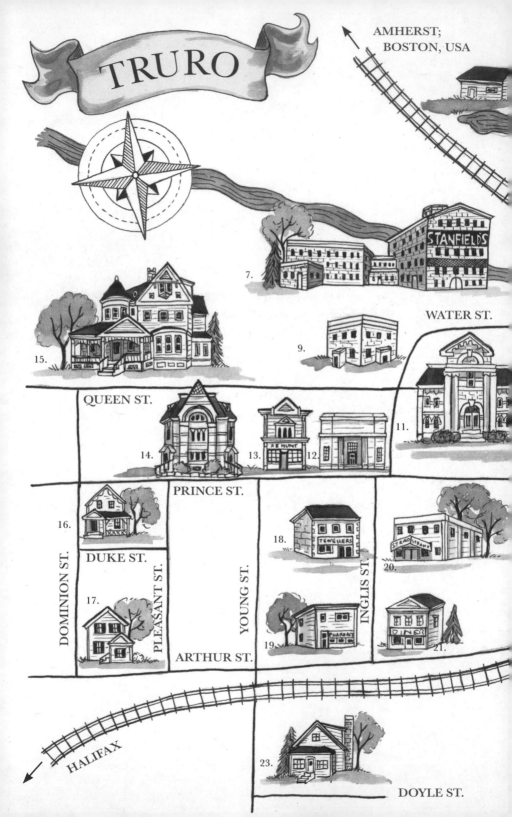

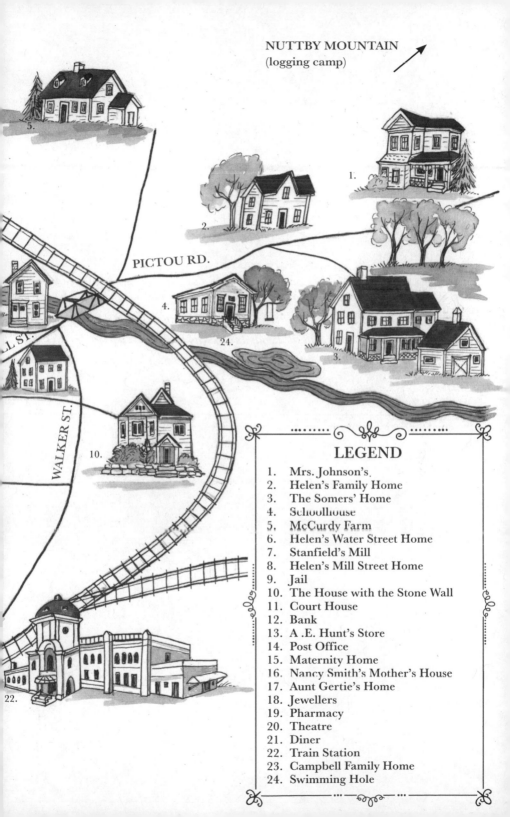

NUTTBY MOUNTAIN
(logging camp)

PICTOU RD.

5.

1.

2.

4.

24.

3.

L ST.

WALKER ST.

10.

22.

LEGEND

1. Mrs. Johnson's
2. Helen's Family Home
3. The Somers' Home
4. Schoolhouse
5. McCurdy Farm
6. Helen's Water Street Home
7. Stanfield's Mill
8. Helen's Mill Street Home
9. Jail
10. The House with the Stone Wall
11. Court House
12. Bank
13. A .E. Hunt's Store
14. Post Office
15. Maternity Home
16. Nancy Smith's Mother's House
17. Aunt Gertie's Home
18. Jewellers
19. Pharmacy
20. Theatre
21. Diner
22. Train Station
23. Campbell Family Home
24. Swimming Hole

This was a small place,
where the wind carried whispers like snowflakes
and all heads turned eagerly
to catch them on their tongues.

Prologue

My mother was not one to dwell on the past. "Digging up old memories is like eating cherries," she said. "Some people choose the sweet ones every time, and then there are the others, those who always choose the sour." She said either way, you were left with a slimy pit in the palm of your hand—*the ghost*, she called it. "No good can come from that."

I don't agree with my mother. I have always liked the sweet and the sour. You really can't appreciate one without the other. Memories are like that, too. Sometimes they're all you have, so you take what you can. When I close my eyes, I can take myself back to that road. I feel the hot sun on my back, I smell the wild roses, I taste the road dust on my tongue, and I hear the children playing in the fields. I see every building I pass and every person who looks my way and I ache with the child in my belly, ready to be born.

That road holds all the ghosts of my life. On every corner, in every building, under every tree, and down every lane, I see them watching me and judging the past. All those I loved and all those I did not. They want to relive it. Stir it up again and see how it will all settle back down, like a child's snow globe.

These memories are the map of my life, each triggered by their own essence, each found on the road I walked over sixty years ago when my baby came and saved my life.

Thunderstorms

Summer 1946

The full force of heaven rained down on us that night. Each rattling crack of thunder was followed by a brief light that held such shocking intensity I could not help but think of my father. When storms shook our tiny cabin in the woods, he held me close and told me not to worry, it was only God clearing his head for tomorrow.

"Good things are coming," he said. "God is getting ready for a special day."

And it was a special day, the day I walked that road. The best memory I have is the day she was born. Mrs. Johnson told me just the week before that I was close. "You've dropped, Helen, it won't be long now." She was excited at the prospect of having a baby in her house once again, and all the joy she knew came with a little one.

At that point I was so naive and scared I did not know what to expect, but I was determined to face it with courage. I had no desire to involve my mother in the birth of my child. She would not understand or accept my decisions. There was no use trying to explain. All I knew was that I needed to be away from the familiar and start living a new life. A life of my own.

Mrs. Johnson was more than happy to rent me a room when I arrived at her door six months earlier, soaking wet, trembling, and unable to speak. *A lost soul* is what she called me that day. And I think she may have been right. But time had done its work and I felt like a new person, two people really, myself and the little one growing inside me. Hope had not been something I was taught as a child, but it was something I now clung to.

At dawn that summer's day, I quietly gathered my bag and crept down the stairs. The weathered floorboards on the old porch were still damp and I paused to look at the long road ahead. Steam rose from the dirt, erasing last night's storm. The fields surrounding the house were lush and green, and the morning dew clung to each blade of grass like stubborn tears. I wore the only coat I had, to cover my large stomach. It was not meant for summer and I knew the coming heat would be unbearable, but it was my only choice. My suitcase weighed me down as I struggled to walk, to keep breathing through the pains that gripped my belly and travelled down my back. I had seven miles to go.

Lingering storm clouds kept the light at bay as I approached the end of Mrs. Johnson's lane. Before turning onto the main road I stopped under the oak trees. I closed my eyes and listened. I could make out the robins, warblers, and thrush as they brought in the new day. I had never heard birds so clearly. Their high-pitched calls and low twittering melodies mingled together to create an air of exciting anticipation. I opened my eyes to search for the morning choir just as the sun started to peak through the clouds. The light was streaming through the outstretched branches, cascading toward the earth. I smiled, remembering the magical shafts of light from my childhood in the woods.

Pine Needles & Shafts of Light

Fall 1921

When I was five years old, my father took our family on an adventure. He called it our Grand Adventure. He packed us up and moved us to the woods—my mother, my older brother, Russell, my younger sister, Eunice, and me. Our new home was in a logging camp six hours' walk from town. *God's country*, Father called it. I spent my first morning in God's country looking for the man himself. I never found Him.

The camp was deep in the woods, surrounded by the tallest trees I had ever seen. Giant maples, towering birch, and monstrous pines loomed over our little cabin like soldiers. I spent most of my days wandering among them, learning the locations of the biggest and most beautiful. It didn't take me long to realize my father was right, this was God's country. He lived among the shafts of light that travelled from the distant heavens to the damp earth. On sunny days, hours disappeared as I lay on the soft forest bed, watching God's lights slip into the woods from high above and then disappear among the trees.

The magic of the woods was lost within our tiny cabin. I hated being inside those old, dark walls. It had only three rooms: the kitchen and sitting area, my parents' bedroom, and the storage room, where Eunie and I slept. There was a woodshed and an outhouse not too far from the back door.

We only saw Russell on Sundays, when he came to visit. He worked and bunked with the logging men in a large, low building about a ten-minute walk from us through a path in the woods. Father ordered us girls never to go there alone. But I often followed him there in the mornings. If he knew I was hiding in the woods, he never let on. I could sit for hours and listen to the men sing as they swung their axes. They were strong, boisterous country boys who loved the fresh air and honest work. Father laughed and joked with them, at ease away from a house full of women. Big Jim, they called him. He was both feared and respected by his men.

He ran the camp as best he could. He hired the men, made sure the lumber orders were filled, and reported the earnings to a man in town we never met. The Man with the Money, my mother called him. Mother looked after the workmen's meals. There was a kitchen in the logging quarters and that is where she spent a good part of her days. Arriving home at dusk, she would slam down the pot containing our dinner and order me to serve it up.

She loathed God's country and spent every waking moment muttering about the filthy godforsaken shack my father had dragged her to. My love of the camp seemed to cause her further frustration. My clothes were always torn and dirty, my thick, curly hair full of burrs and unknown matter, and my freckled skin red and raw from fly bites. She hated to see me coming; I tried my best to stay away.

Eunie loved being inside the cabin with my mother. She was almost three years younger than me, and she refused to play in the woods or get herself dirty. She was Mama's pet. I was Daddy's. Russell seemed to float somewhere in between—coddled by my mother and protected by my father. This family dynamic stuck to us like feathers on molasses.

Later in the lumber season, when the days were longer, my mother prepared night lunches for my father. Just as the sun was setting, she would tell me to go through the path and deliver it. I may have loved those woods in the day, but the evenings were different. I was scared. Petrified is more like it, and she knew it. The first time I refused her I was only seven years old. "Don't make me go, Mama," I begged. "There are bears in the woods at night, please don't make me go in the dark."

She stormed out the back door and tore a switch from an alder bush. She gave no threats or second chances. Before I could blink, I felt the sting of five quick lashes on my backside. "Get going, girl."

Tears still streaming, the lunch in one hand and the kerosene lamp in the other, I set off, eyes darting this way and that on the lookout for bears. Shadow and moonlight replaced God's lights and the noises of the forest were foreign. I reached my father's welcoming smile at the other end of the path and couldn't remember how I got there. The sweet smell of sawdust filled my nose as he wrapped his large arms around me and told me what a good girl I was. He always made me feel protected and safe. One hug from him could erase a day of misery with Mother.

I don't know if he ever learned about the alder switch. But that night, and all that followed, Father had Russell walk me home through the woods. Russell was already fifteen, almost a real man. He would hold the light in one hand and my hand in the other and we would walk back in silence.

It was a cold, damp night in late October when life at the lumber camp changed. I was walking through the heavy mist, taking the night lunch to my father, when Russell appeared just before I reached the other side of the path. I could see the faint lights of the men's quarters, and I could hear men arguing. My father's voice was above them all. "Anyone else got anything to say?" he yelled. "You'll end up just like this one."

"What's wrong, Russell? Why's Daddy angry, what's happened?"

Russell's eyes were wide and wild. His cheeks were streaked with dirt, blood, and tears. His shirt was ripped and stained. I thought I could see blood on his hands. He looked terrified. "Hurry, Helen." He grabbed my arm and turned me back toward our cabin. "We need to fetch a doctor."

"Is Daddy hurt, Russell?" I held my breath as my brother's fear worked its way into my little body.

"No, one of the men is hurt bad." He started to run. "We've got to fetch the doctor."

As Russell pulled me through the woods that night, the only sound I could register was the whipping and snapping of branches as they tore at my face and legs. My heart pounded with an unknown fear. It felt like I was flying, my feet barely touching the ground as my brother ran toward our cabin, towing me behind him like an unwanted appendage. When we arrived at the cabin Russell leaned on the kitchen table, gripping its edges as he gasped for air, his body shaking.

"We need a doctor." I managed to get the words out first.

"What's happened?" demanded Mother, tugging at his arm. "Why do you need the doctor? Who's hurt?" Russell turned and shoved her back into her chair.

"Shut up." Russell's voice was a low, slow growl. His eyes wild. "I can't stand to look at you. This man's beating is on you!" He spat the words through gritted teeth, blood and spittle dripping down his chin as he pounded the kitchen table. I stood in shock as he walked out the door and slammed it behind him. Russell never raised his voice to our mother. I had never seen him this upset or angry. Mother fell quiet. Her face lost all colour and her mouth tightened as I watched her stare at the door.

"Mama?"

We both turned to see Eunie standing in the shadows at the back of the room. She rubbed her eyes, her tiny hands knotted into fists. "I'm scared," she said, her small, quivering voice on the verge of tears. My mother had no comforting words for Eunie that day; she simply turned back to the door where Russell had disappeared. I had no idea what was happening, but I knew enough to keep my mouth shut.

Father's knuckles were raw the next day. Mother hid his shirt under the laundry pile, but I saw it, covered in blood. I knew Mother must have had something to do with that night because Russell acted differently toward her after that. He ignored her and she seemed to be nervous around him, trying to please him on the rare times he came up from the men's quarters.

I knew the details of that night would never be discussed, but my curiosity would not let it go. Over the next few weeks I hid in the woods during the days and listened in on the men working. I heard bits and pieces: "...a beating from Big Jim...almost killed him... raising a bastard...young Russell should've stayed out of it...Robert's boy...if you want to work, keep your mouth shut."

My father never spoke of that night. On Sundays, when my mother asked him where Russell was, my father simply said, "Leave it be." Normally it was my mother's anger and raging moods that kept us on edge, but this was new. She was worried about something and I could sense Father did not want her, or us, asking questions. Though I missed my walks with Russell, I could not help but be a little bit happy, as I was never asked to take night lunch again.

Freshly Cut Spruce

Winter 1923

I saw her breath hit the air before I could make out her face. My mother. She was wrapped in an old wool blanket, grey with faded red stripes and tiny moth holes along the edges. She entered our room slowly, the creaks in the floorboards announcing her arrival.

Eunie and I slept in the same bed, a narrow squeaking beast that poked and prodded us endlessly with its rusting springs. The bed was pushed into a corner of the back room behind the kitchen. I slept on the outside and Eunie was against the wall. My mother's left hand clutched the blanket under her chin as she approached the bed. I could see a lump under the blanket where her right hand was concealing something. *This is it*, I thought, *our presents*. I wished Father were here to watch us open them and I decided to run and find him. I sat up and was instantly shoved back down by my mother's rough hand. Her blanket fell to the floor and she pushed her face before mine. The stale, familiar smell hit me like an iron fist. "Girls that snoop don't get nothing for Christmas." She reached over me and handed Eunie a beautiful porcelain doll. "Merry Christmas, Eunie," she muttered then turned, leaving us to stare at the back of her dingy white nightshirt.

Burying my face in the pillow, I bit the inside of my cheek, the metallic bitter taste of blood filling my mouth. *I will not cry*, I told myself, *I will not cry*. Eunie climbed over me and ran into the main room, clutching her doll and singing Christmas carols to herself. I got out of bed, reached down for the old blanket, and wrapped myself in it. I followed Eunie. She was at the table, eating her breakfast and playing with her new doll. Father wasn't home. Mother stood at the stove frying bread, her back to me. There was a fully decorated Christmas tree in front of the window where a small table had been just the night before. I walked over to the tree slowly and that's when I saw it. A doll, almost as nice as Eunie's, with a tag that read, *For Helen*. My first doll. I let the blanket fall to the ground and took the doll from the tree. The smell of freshly cut spruce filled my nose. How long had I waited for this moment? A real Christmas, with a real tree and a real present. But as I stared at the doll, I felt nothing. I went to the table, placed the doll face down before me, and ate my cold oatmeal. My mother did not speak to me the entire day and I had no idea where my father was.

"Time to take that tree down," my mother said. It was the third morning after Christmas.

"Can't we just wait, so Daddy can see it?" I asked.

She stood in front of the tree, her face hard and angry. "I want it gone," she said. "He doesn't care about Christmas or us. Did you see him here for Christmas? Do you see him here with his family? Did he decorate this tree?"

I kept my head down, staring at my feet. Eunie and I gently took the few ornaments off the tree and put them in boxes with little cardboard compartments, each ball nestled in its own protective square. When the tree was bare, my mother and I dragged it out the door and over the snow to the edge of the woods.

"What's this, Christmas is over already?" My father's voice echoed in the cool air. Mother and I both jumped in surprise. He stood at the entrance to the path which led to the road. His high boots were lost beneath the snow and he was not wearing a proper coat for the cold weather. I ran to him but stopped when I saw his face. His right eye was almost swollen shut and a deep purple bruise spread down his cheek. His bottom lip was cut and caked with dried blood. His clothes were crumpled and dirty. "There's my girl," he said, bending down to welcome me into his arms. A light breeze blew the smell off him and I almost gagged. He stank of liquor and urine. I turned to run into the house, tears in my eyes.

"Take a good look, Helen," my mother yelled. "This is your daddy, home from the drunken brawl that landed him in jail on Christmas Eve." I kept running past her and slammed the cabin door behind me. My parents stayed outside arguing. I lay face down on my bed with the pillow over my head. Eunie came in and got under the covers with her doll. I could feel her reaching for my hand.

"What's happening, Helen?" she whispered. I took her hand, and we heard the door open and close. Father's steps were the only sound in the cabin and I listened as he stumbled around, opening and closing cupboards and drawers. He approached our room and we remained still. I kept the pillow over my head and felt his large, warm hand rest on my back. The three of us felt connected for just a short moment, and then he removed his hand. I heard his boots scrape across the floor and then the door opened and quietly shut. I knew he was gone.

I found the winter nights desperately long. I missed my father. During the days I escaped to the woods and spent hours playing in the deep snowdrifts. But the winter sun was not as kind as the summer, and I found no comfort without God's lights. For weeks he stayed away. Mother told us he was bunking with Russell in the camp quarters. Then he started visiting us once a week. We sat at the table and practiced my letters and numbers like we used to. It was my favourite thing. He brought old newspapers and I used a piece of charcoal to write. The powdery black dust lingered for days around the table, a constant reminder of him.

"You need to learn to read and write," he said. "My father could do neither and he worked himself dead before he was fifty, farming and labouring. I had to leave school in grade five to help my mother, and I want my girls to get a real education."

"Then get them out of this godforsaken camp," my mother yelled, throwing the pot she was cleaning on the floor. "Let us live somewhere they can go to school and we can have a decent life outside these four miserable walls."

"I make my living here." He kept his eyes on the old newspapers on the table.

"Well, your family won't be here," she said. "Helen will be starting school in September come hell or high water, and we'll be moving somewhere near town to make that happen, with or without you."

I looked from my father to my mother. She stood behind him, glaring at his back, hands balled into tight little fists against her thighs. His large hands lay flat on the table, his fingers spread wide. "Write another line, Helen, you're doing good," he said. "You were made for learning."

Soon after that my father was back staying in the cabin again, sleeping in his own bed with my mother. Some nights he came home late, and if he was smelling of liquor my mother made him leave again. "I'll not have it, I won't," she yelled. I listened from my bed and wondered why he had to go and make her so mad, and why couldn't she just ignore him and let him go to sleep. I was in a constant state of waiting. Waiting for him to come home, then waiting for her to make him leave, which she inevitably would.

There was no tenderness between them. They shared a bed, but nothing else. I did catch a glimpse of something once. Mother had burned her hand on the cast iron pan while cooking breakfast. Father leaped up, knocked over his chair, and rushed to her side. His hands gently cupped hers and his lips almost touched her fingers as he blew cool air on her wounds. Her face softened, just for an instant, as she let him tend to her. She looked over at Eunie and I sitting at the table in our old torn nightshirts, our eyes wide at such a rare sight. "Let me be, for God's sake." She batted him away, her cheeks flushed. "You think I don't burn myself when you're not around? I don't need you helping me." Off she stormed to the bedroom, leaving my father standing in the middle of the kitchen as the bacon burned in the pan.

Spring and summer slid by in the midst of the working and fighting. I retreated to the woods, but the magic was slowly disappearing. I did not feel the same comfort in the smells and shadows as I had just months earlier. The light I had always sought on my walks was fading, and I was left with a lonely darkness. I felt betrayed by my one place of refuge. By the end of August, my mother said we were moving.

"Is Daddy coming?" I asked.

"Your father will be living with us when he can. He has work here. He'll help us move in the fall."

"Will I go to school?" I held my breath, eager for the answer I dreamed of.

"You'll be going to school," she said. "Eunie will stay home with me and start her schooling next year."

I was elated.

Little White Schoolhouses

Fall 1924

In the fall, when the trees of the forest shed their last leaves, and God's lights were harder to find, I said goodbye to the woods. We moved to a small house just outside the nearest town, a place called Truro. I don't know who owned the house, but Mother said it was to be our home. It stood on the edge of the road, leaning slightly to the left, with peeling white paint and cracked windows. It had an upstairs, real bedrooms, and the fanciest outhouse I'd ever seen: a two-seater, so you never had to wait.

Father helped us move and stayed with us for two days. "This is my busy time," he said. "I have to get back to the camp." Mother made our first big meal in the new house so that we could have a proper dinner at noon before he left. While she was cooking, Father found me exploring in the woods behind the house. The scattered, stunted trees made no impression on me. They were not the giants from the camp woods. I wondered if everything would be different here.

"Let's go see this new school of yours," he said.

"Will it be open today?" I asked.

"No, but we can take a look. It will be like practice, so you'll know where to go your first day." He pulled the watch out of his pocket. I looked at him expectantly and he handed it to me. This was our ritual. I was allowed to press the little button on top that opened its round door to reveal the time.

I loved that watch. It was the finest thing we owned. My father had won it in a bet. It was silver and had the initials *F.T.S.* on the back. He always joked "Let's ask Frank the time" when he pulled it from his pocket. Today he did not joke about Frank, he simply handed the watch to me and I told him the time. He took my hand and we started down the road. There were not many neighbours, but the few we did see, my father greeted with a large "Good day" as we walked by. His long legs strutted like he owned the world. I walked with my head held high and smiled at anyone who looked our way. I felt like I had the biggest, strongest Daddy in the entire world.

The schoolhouse was as special as I had imagined. It was a perfect rectangle with a high, pitched roof and it stood in a large, cleared field. The shiny white paint gleamed in the sunshine and the large windows, which seemed to stretch from floor to ceiling, were trimmed in black. It stood on the same road as our house, but on the opposite side. There was a row of trees along the roadside and one giant oak had a swing hanging from it. My father took out his watch again and handed it to me. I pressed the little button. "How long did it take us?" he asked.

I looked at the time and quickly replied, "Twenty-five minutes."

"Now you know how long it'll be taking you to get here every morning," he said.

I ran to the tire and climbed up. "Push me, Daddy."

He came over, smiling. "Hold on tight." He pushed me higher and higher. I leaned back and looked up through the tree. The sun was shining through the branches and if I squinted really hard, I thought I could make out a few God's lights. Father smiled up at me and I let him keep pushing, wishing we could stay like this forever.

On the walk home he told me to work hard at school and be a good girl, to help my mother with the chores after school. "Your mother is right. You should be going to school and not living in the woods," he said.

"I love the woods," I said.

"That's 'cause you're my girl." He gave my hand a little squeeze. "I'm going to come visit you girls as much as I can," he said. "But you'll see, once you start reading all kinds of books and learning all your history, you won't even miss me."

I kept my head down. There was a lump growing in my throat and I could feel tears coming to my eyes. I wanted to tell him I would always miss him and that I loved him. But we never said things like that, and I knew if I spoke I would start to cry. I was a big girl now, so I squeezed my eyes shut and kept walking.

My first morning of school my mother fussed over me for the first time in my life. I was scrubbed like the kitchen floor. My hair was combed, my dress ironed, and I was given a lunch. As I went out the door, she grabbed my arm. "People can say you have a no-good drunken father, but they'll never say your mother didn't take care of you. You remember that." I kept my head down and stared at my worn shoes. "You're representing your mother and you best always be looking clean and acting proper."

"Yes, Mother." I started down the road as fast as my feet would take me. It was hard to know whether I was more excited about going to school, or leaving my mother behind. She had started to take in laundry, saying we couldn't rely on Father for money. So, I knew my time at school would be only a brief escape from my chores. Soon enough I would be home again, elbow-deep in suds, scrubbing some stranger's shirts.

I could hear the bell ringing as I crossed the road and approached the little schoolhouse. I told myself I would have to walk faster tomorrow so I wouldn't be late. The other children all broke free from their little groups and ran toward the stairs. I could feel my stomach tightening as I came up behind them. I was nervous but happy to be the last to enter the school.

I walked through the door and was greeted by a flurry of ribbons and curls. "I'm Madge Somers, you're new, aren't you? What's your name? How old are you?" She bounced from one foot to the other and smiled her big white grin. She had the prettiest hair, like pure sunshine, and her eyes were blue like robins' eggs. She wore a bright pink dress and shiny black shoes. I simply stared at her.

A proper-looking lady appeared at the front of the room and asked us all to take our seats. Her hair was pulled back in a bun and not one strand was out of place. She stood with her shoulders tall and straight and her dress was crisp and clean, not one wrinkle to be found. She looked happy and serious at the same time. I wanted to reach out and touch her, to make sure she was real.

Madge took my hand and led me down the aisle. I could see there were four rows of desks, but I dared not look around. "You'll sit with me," Madge said.

There were initials and partial words and numbers carved into the wood. I traced them with my finger and wondered if I was expected to write my name on the desk. When the teacher began to speak, I looked up and saw a large map of the world hanging behind her. I had never seen a real map before, only the kind my father had drawn for me. I could see Africa and China. China! Right there on the wall. I wondered what little girls were doing in China right now. Were they learning to read? And what about the little girls in Africa, what were they doing on a warm October day? Did they all go to little white schoolhouses? Madge nudged me and pointed to the teacher. "Helen McNutt, I asked if you could come up to my desk, please." My tummy knotted. *I'm in trouble already. I haven't learned one thing yet, and I've been called up to the teacher's desk. Mother will be furious.*

I walked to the front of the room where the teacher sat behind her desk, facing the class. "I'm Miss MacMillan, Helen," she said. I nodded and my fingers reached out and touched the top of her pretty blue desk. She had an inkwell, a large book with names written in it, the school bell, and a leather strap all sitting on it. I pulled my hand back and stared at the leather strap. My mother had told me about the strap. Miss MacMillan brought a stool over and asked me to sit beside her. "Because this is your first day, Helen, I thought we could go over a few letters and numbers, so I will have a better idea of what grade you should be starting." *What grade?* I should be in grade two. What was she talking about? I stayed silent. I knew you were never to talk back to the teacher.

I kept my eyes on the strap as she started to ask me questions and simple math problems. Then she asked me to read a little piece of paper about a girl and her baby calf. I read the paper and then she handed me a slate and asked me to write my name and the words *Nova Scotia* and *Canada*. I did as I was told. "And you've never gone to school, Helen?" I shook my head. "Well, someone has taught you very well," she said.

I could not contain my proud smile. "My father."

"You may go back and sit with Madge now," she said. "You will do your studies with Madge and the other grade two students." I sat with Madge while Miss MacMillan wrote lessons on the board and answered questions from other students, mostly the girls. I was still thinking about what she had said about my father teaching me well when she stood and rang her bell. "Recess," she called out, and the room came to life again.

Madge grabbed my hand and pulled me toward the door.

"Who's your new friend, Madge? Freckle-face?" A redheaded boy wearing no shoes stood in front of me.

"This is my friend, Helen McNutt. And in case you haven't noticed, Davey Dewar, you've got freckles all over your own nose!" Davey stuck his tongue out at us and ran down the stairs with the other boys. Madge reached out and quickly touched my cheek. It felt like a butterfly brushing its wings against my skin. "My mother says freckles are beauty spots. I really like your freckles. I wish I had more. I just have the one, here on my arm, see?" She held her arm up to my face and I could see a tiny mole next to her elbow. I had never thought about my freckles before. I touched my cheek and looked at Madge's face. It was pure white, not a mark anywhere, not even any colour from the sun. "Let's swing," she said. We ran over to the oak tree. "You go first." I climbed on the tire and she started pushing me.

That was the beginning. Madge was my first friend and from that day on we were inseparable. At eight years old, I was like an old sponge, all dried up from lack of giggles and girlish silliness. When I met Madge, I was ready to absorb all she had to offer. No two children could have been more different, in dress, manner, and looks. It didn't matter. Where she led, I followed. She filled my lungs with a new kind of air, and I thought she was the most exciting thing that had ever happened to me.

My first day of school was a success and I carried a new sense of belonging home with me that day. I felt I was now a small part of the world and I was grateful to my father for ensuring I'd fit in. "How did you do?" my mother asked when I walked into the house. She was making bread and did not look up as I placed my lunch pail on the table. Eunie sat at the table playing with her doll. She didn't look up at me either.

"The teacher told me Daddy taught me very well."

Mother stopped kneading the dough for a moment and we looked at each other. Her shoulders sagged and her face looked tired and worn. The bitterness from the woods had followed her here, and now rested in her steely blue eyes. Her flour-covered hands hung in mid-air and I waited for her to say something. I was proud of my father for teaching me so well. I knew she could not acknowledge it. She looked back at the table and started kneading the dough again.

"Change your clothes," she said. "You can help me with the laundry out back."

I put on my old dress and went to my mother's room looking for her mirror. It had been a long time since I'd looked at myself. I found it on her dresser, sitting between the glass of water that held her comb and a small jar of cream. I lifted the mirror by the heavy silver handle and examined the pretty lace cover on the back. I traced the lace with my fingers, then turned the glass toward me. I saw a new face looking back. She had thick, frizzy black hair, tiny green eyes too close together, freckles spreading from forehead to chin, and thin little lips. I pulled back my lips in a grimace and looked at my teeth. They were almost straight and mostly yellow except the two missing on the bottom. I put the mirror back gently with the glass facing down. I decided then and there, I was ugly.

Al Jolson
& Strawberry Candy

M y days now felt complete. I had school and I had Madge. I loved them both. "I wish we were sisters," Madge said as she stopped to pick cattails along the side of the road. We now walked home from school together. She lived off Millers Diversion, a road halfway between my house and the school.

"Wouldn't that be great?" I said. "You're much more fun than Eunie, and we could live at your house and share a room. We could even get a kitten." Madge's step slowed.

"Better to live at your house," she said. Her eyebrows were all scrunched up and she wasn't smiling anymore. "We would definitely live at your house, Helen." She stared at me with a distant sadness in her eyes. It was a new look, not something I had seen before. She was not angry, like my mother often looked. She was not even upset. It was something I could not quite place.

"Okay, we could live at my house." I said. I didn't want to disappoint her. With a look of relief, she ran past me to chase a dragonfly.

"Come on, Helen!" She pumped her legs faster and faster. I chased after her. I would do anything to make her happy.

Later that night, I lay beside Eunie in our cramped little bed. My father had returned for one of his visits. I listened to my mother nattering at him about the lack of money, and the endless clink of the bottle against his glass. I thought about Madge and wondered why anyone would choose to live in this house. I did like the idea of her being my sister though. Until I met Madge, I had thought

Eunie and I were the way sisters were meant to be. But now that I knew the joy and comradery that could exist between girls, I knew Eunie and I would never be close. We had no bond. She was like an extension of my mother. It was hard to say if this was my mother's doing, by making Eunie the favourite and treating us so differently, but in the end that was how it was. She was a part of my life, but I felt she really had no effect on me.

It wasn't long before Madge took me to her house after school. She lived in a large home with fancy furniture and real paintings on the wall. They had gardens with stone seats for people to sit outside. I could not imagine my mother and father sitting in a garden under a shady tree sipping drinks. But that is just what Madge and I did that first day. A housekeeper named Mrs. Parsons brought us apple cider on a silver tray with some cookies. She seemed very interested in me. Madge told her I was Helen McNutt, her best friend.

"And who would your father be now, Helen?" she asked.

"James," I said quietly, almost cautiously. I had an uneasy feeling this was some kind of test, and no matter what my answers, I was going to fail.

"James," she repeated slowly. "James McNutt. I just can't place that name. And what does he do, your father?"

"He works in the lumber camp." I brushed some crumbs off my lap and looked up at her raised eyebrows. "He runs it for another man," I added this last bit, thinking this was somehow a better answer.

"Well, that sounds exciting, doesn't it?" she said. "And he must be gone a lot then, working at a lumber camp. Are you a good help to your mother?"

"Yes," I said.

"And what is your mother's name?"

"Blanche."

"Blanche?" She knotted her brow in concentration.

"Yes," I said again.

"Blanche Reid?" she asked.

"No, her name is Blanche McNutt," I said. "Just like me."

"Of course, dear, of course." She smiled and told us not to get dirty playing outside, and started back to the house. She stopped and quickly turned to me again, "You've an older brother, Helen," she said. It was more of a statement than a question.

"Yes, Russell," I said. "And my younger sister is Eunice." Another nod and she was gone.

"She's a busybody, that Mrs. Parsons," whispered Madge. "Always asking questions and telling other people the answers." I knew right away I did not like Mrs. Parsons or her questions.

I was not allowed to go to Madge's house very often. My mother liked me to come home and do chores or watch after Eunie while she did her errands. Eunie really was not that much of a bother; she tended to play on her own inside and always did what she was told. Of course, when I was Eunie's age, no one was watching after me. In fact, I was doing laundry and delivering night lunch when I was Eunie's age. But I was Helen.

I'd been to Madge's house five times before I saw her mother. Madge said she had headaches and liked to stay in her room and rest. The first time she came into the kitchen I was awestruck. "Here's my sweetness," she said, cupping Madge's face in her hands and kissing her on the forehead. "And, you must be Helen, the best friend who I have heard so much about." She walked over and gave me a tight hug while I sat on my stool at the kitchen table.

"Hello, Mrs. Somers," I said.

She stepped back and placed her index finger on the tip of my nose. "You call me Kit," she said. Great piles of curly blond hair were piled on top of her head, the odd curl escaping down her back like a golden spring. Her skin was clear and white just like Madge's, and she smelled like lilacs. Her dress was a deep green and when she moved it swished and swayed. I had only seen that colour in the early spring forest where the moss grew thick and lush. She turned the radio on and grabbed Madge's hands. Al Jolson floated above us, belting out promises of a faraway land. "California, Here I Come!" Madge giggled and threw her head back as her mother twirled her around the kitchen table in her bare feet. They sang to the music and wove their way around the room with ease. I watched them with a mixture of disbelief and envy.

The song ended and Kit flopped down in a chair beside me. She propped her elbows on the table and rested her chin in her hands. She smiled at me with her perfect white teeth. "Let's play cards!" she said. I stared into her eyes. One was blue, like Madge's, and the other was a pale brown. Both held a deep sadness that wouldn't let them sparkle. It was not the same sadness I saw in my mother's eyes when my father would come home with the liquor smell, or not come home at all; this was a different kind of sad, the kind I had seen in Madge's eyes when she said she wanted to live at my house. From that day on I always checked Madge's mother's eyes. But no matter how big her smile, or how loud her laugh, she couldn't make her sad eyes sparkle.

The second time I saw her mother was a rainy November day. Madge and I were cutting out dresses for her paper dolls. Mrs. Somers lay on the carpet between me and Madge in the large living room. She was on her back, her dressed hiked up almost to her garters and her hair fanned out around her head like an angel's halo. Her eyes were closed and she hummed a song I did not recognize. Madge and I were on our tummies facing the fireplace, its warm glow keeping the room nice and cozy. "You girls have your whole lives ahead of you," she said. "You are so lucky. You make sure you do some exciting things and go far away from this little place to somewhere where there are lots of people, all kinds of different people."

"What kinds of people would you look for, Katherine?" The soft, firm voice startled all three of us and Mrs. Somers bolted up, pushed her skirt down below her knees, and smoothed her hair down as much as possible. Madge turned to face her father and gave him a big smile.

"Why are you home, Daddy?" He stood with his arms folded, looking down on us. He was a short, round man with not a hair on his head except for his bushy black eyebrows. He wore a dark blue suit and a tie. Madge had told me he worked at an office in town.

"Well, some days I just have a feeling that I am needed at home, Madge. And who is this?" he said, looking at me.

"This is Helen McNutt, Daddy. I told you all about her."

"Very nice to meet you, Miss McNutt," he said, stooping over to shake my hand. "I hope Mrs. Somers isn't filling your head with silly ideas."

"No sir," I said, placing my hand in his as he lightly shook it. He reached into his pocket and pulled out two lollipops. He held them out, one in each hand. I had never seen a lollipop so big. My eyes travelled up from the lollipop to his face. Then I saw his smile. His two front teeth were pure gold and the light from the fire danced around his mouth. Madge jumped up and took the candy. I stayed on the carpet, unsure of what to do. Mrs. Somers remained sitting, staring at her bare toes.

"Don't be shy, Helen," he said, giving me a wink. I rose slowly and took the lollipop.

"Thank you, Mr. Somers," I said.

"Two good girls deserve two good treats, don't you think?" he said. We nodded and licked our lollipops, our tongues turning red from the strawberry flavour.

Mrs. Somers rose to her feet. Her face had turned pale and she held her fingers against her temples. "I must go lie down." She said it so softly I could hardly make her out.

"Yes, Katherine, you look like you are coming down with a headache. Best you go rest," he said. As she left the room, she briefly placed a hand on each of our heads. I did not want to look up into her eyes. I knew what I would see. I could feel it in the air, the same way I could feel the storm clouds over my own house when my mother came in to find us laughing with my father. I looked up at Mrs. Somers and she smiled down at me, but her eyes told me she had already gone somewhere else, somewhere you couldn't hum snappy dance songs.

Mr. Somers took his wife's elbow and led her out of the room and up the stairs. "Daddy doesn't like Mama to talk about other places," Madge whispered.

"Why not?" I asked.

Madge shrugged. "Mama would like to live in town where there are more people, but Daddy says he likes the country."

"The country?" I said, forgetting to whisper. "We live in town!"

"This is not really town, Helen," Madge said. "Mama says we are living like country bumpkins."

I shook my head slowly. If this was the country, I wondered where I had been living before. We lay back down in front of the fire and licked our treats in silence. Madge kept glancing at the staircase as if she were expecting someone to come back. I wondered what life would be like living in this big house with a fun mother and a father who wore a suit and tie.

"Your father seems very nice, Madge," I said, even though I sensed a darkness in his presence. "Do you get treats like this all the time?"

"Yes." She licked her lollipop slowly. "Daddy likes to keep us happy. He's always rewarding us for being good."

I did not see either of Madge's parents again that day. But I thought of her father as I threw up great gushes of red strawberry in the bushes on my walk home.

High Heels & Hugs

Playing with Madge and dreaming of exciting futures in faraway places was the best time spent. Eunie sometimes followed us around, but her interest was weak and she preferred to be close to Mother. Our lives were quiet and for the most part, time was marked by my father's visits.

Not long after we moved to town, I came home from school to find a car outside. More surprising than finding my mother sitting at the kitchen table laughing with another woman, was finding out that woman was a relative. My mother explained that our aunt, my father's sister, lived only a few miles away. Gertie was her name. She was married to a man named Johnny. We had an aunt and an uncle! I could not remember my parents ever speaking about having brothers or sisters. We had never met any relatives—not a single grandparent, aunt, uncle, or cousin.

I was quite literally speechless as I took in the woman sitting at our table. She had curly red hair and the largest bosom I had ever seen. She wore bright lipstick and lots of jewelry—coloured beads, drooping earrings, and rows of bracelets. Her smile was as natural as the morning sun, and it lit up the room as she laughed at my shocked expression. "I guess our Jim never let on he had a sister by the look on this one's face," she said.

My mother shook her head and took me by the arm, pulling me closer to the table. "Say hello to your aunt Gertie, Helen."

Eunie was standing beside my mother, pasted to the side of her chair, her head hanging down shyly but her eyes peeking up to take in this new stranger. The teacups were half full and Aunt Gertie was smoking a cigarette, but there were no other butts in the ashtray so I figured I hadn't missed much of her visit. "Hello," I said. I couldn't help but smile at her as I could see the resemblance to my father. They had the same eyes.

"How was school today, Helen?" She took both my hands and held them while she talked to me. "Are you as smart as your daddy? He was always the smart one in our house."

"I like school," I said, not wanting to brag about how well I did.

"And I'll bet you're at the top of your class." She gave me a wink and laughed again as she took another drag of her cigarette. "This one's got the hair, doesn't she?" She pulled Eunie up on her lap and admired her fine blond hair. "You're just the cutest thing." She squeezed Eunie closer, almost smothering her in her large bosom. I moved off to the side of the kitchen. "Don't you worry, Helen." It was like she read my mind. "You're going to be a beauty one day. I can tell. Just you wait and see, Blanche. She'll be turning heads when she's older." My mother raised her brows and looked over at me. She looked skeptical. I was pleased and devastated at the same time. My fears were confirmed: I was ugly. But I was given hope, should Aunt Gertie's prediction come true.

In no time our shyness was gone. Aunt Gertie let Eunie and I wear her jewelry and walk around the house in her high-heeled shoes. It was far better than any Christmas Day we had ever had. My mother and Aunt Gertie laughed at us teetering around the kitchen. It was like a fresh breeze had blown in through our window. I had never seen my mother laugh and gossip with another woman. It was strange and exciting at the same time. I felt a kind of relief to see her so at ease. No laundry was done that day. Aunt Gertie talked like the summer rain, long and steady. She told us about every person who lived on the road, who they were related to, what their fathers did, how bad their children were, how much the men drank, who the women gossiped with, and who they owed money to.

Gertie became a regular visitor. There was no explanation as to why we hadn't met her before. I assumed it was because we had lived in the woods, where people didn't visit. She quickly became my second-best friend, behind Madge of course. She had no children of her own. Her husband, Uncle Johnny, became a visitor too. The first time I met him he called Aunt Gertie Collie. "Look at that red hair," he said in his thick Irish accent. "She's my Irish lass. The first time I saw her, she was Colleen to me." He grabbed her and gave her a big kiss on the lips, right in front of us all.

"I'm as Irish as that chair," she laughed, gently pushing him away.

If Uncle Johnny didn't need the car, Aunt Gertie loved to come over and give us the news. Every visit started with a hug for Eunie and me. She would pull us both in at once, crushed against her soft bosom and buried in the smell of her perfume. I think Eunie found it overwhelming, but I loved every minute. Sometimes she took us for a drive to town where we could get penny candy at the store. My mother was content, and that made life better for all of us. We even had Uncle Johnny and Aunt Gertie for Sunday dinner every once in a while.

Months and seasons passed at a speed unworthy of any childhood. My father continued to visit over the next year, usually one weekend a month. He was like an unpredictable wind. He blew in like a warm thunder squall, charged with excitement and havoc, then departed, a weakened breeze leaving a lonely emptiness in his wake. He still drank when he came and would share a bottle with Uncle Johnny on the rare occasion, but there were no more nights of fights and drunkenness or jail visits—at least none that I was aware of.

Russell never came to see us, but my mother asked endless questions about him during my father's visits. "The boy is doing fine" was his normal response. She had a nervous habit of rubbing the scar behind her right ear when she worried. When she spoke of Russell, she would stroke the scar absentmindedly. Once, when I was brushing her hair, I asked her how she got such a large jagged scar, but she said it must have happened when she was a little girl because she really couldn't remember.

My mother was more relaxed with her new life in town, and although they did not embrace one another or give playful kisses like Uncle Johnny and Aunt Gertie sometimes did, she and my father seemed to quietly tolerate each other. After dinner one Sunday night, I asked my father if he could stay one more day so that he could finally meet Madge.

"Who's this now, Helen?" Aunt Gertie asked.

"Madge is my best friend from school," I said.

"Well, why haven't I heard of her before?" Aunt Gertie sat up straighter in her chair and leaned in closer to me. "What's her last name?"

"Somers," I said.

"From up Millers Diversion?" she asked.

"Yes," I said.

"My, my," she said. "I didn't know you were hobnobbing with the likes of Kit Somers. Up in that fancy house, while her son lives over a garage."

"What son?" I asked.

My father, who was not a fan of gossip, interrupted before she could answer. "I wish I could meet your friend, but I have to leave later tonight. Why don't you go fetch your reader and show me your school work." He gave his sister a stern look and no more was said about Kit Somers that day.

That night, my father handed my mother money as he usually did and said his goodbyes. It was three months before we saw him again.

Water Spiders & Monthlies

Spring 1925

Madge and I arrived at her house after school one day to find Mrs. Parsons's daughter, Eloise, sitting in the kitchen reading one of Mrs. Somers's magazines. Eloise was a heavy girl, with crooked teeth and mousy brown hair.

"Hello girls," Mrs. Parsons greeted us. She gushed about our pretty hair and asked what we had learned in school. She explained Eloise was out of school with a tummy ache and had come to stay for the day. "But you're feeling much better now, aren't you Eloise?" Mrs. Parsons asked. Eloise wrinkled her nose. "Why don't you go play with the girls for a while and I will bake you all some cookies."

Eloise reluctantly rose from her chair and came outside with us. We all walked down by the pond and sat to watch the water spiders skip across the water. Eloise grabbed her tummy a couple of times. She looked miserable.

"Are you feeling sick?" Madge asked.

"I'm not sick," she said. "I got The Curse."

"What curse?" Madge and I asked at the same time.

"You don't know about The Curse?" Her eyebrows raised just like her mother's did when she asked a question she already knew the answer to. We both shook our heads. "When a girl is twelve, she starts to bleed from *down there*," she said, pointing, "in your private spots. It's called The Curse, and it means you are now a woman." Eloise spoke in a slow, serious tone, watching our faces closely. She gave every detail she could about The Curse, which she said some women also called monthlies. She told us we would have this bleeding curse every single month of our lives, until we were old and the curse-blood in our bodies all dried up.

"You will get stomach cramps too," she said. "That's why it is called The Curse, which sounds about right, because it also means you can now have a baby. But not alone. It takes a boy and a girl to have a baby. If a boy puts his pecker in the hole *down there*, the one where the blood comes out," she said, pointing again, "it makes a baby grow. Then when the baby is too big to stay inside, it comes right out that same hole where the blood came. And this isn't the hole you pee out of either. It is an entirely different hole. You have three down there—one for pee, one for poop, and one for peckers. That third hole must be like magic, cause one minute it fits a pecker, and the next an entire baby can crawl right out of there!"

My eyes were wide with shock. My mouth hung open and I could not speak. I had never heard such talk in my life. I turned in disbelief to Madge. She stood and glared down at Eloise. Her cheeks were now burning red. "That can't be true," she said. "How do you know all of this?"

"My sisters told me," Eloise said. "They've already got The Curse. One even has a baby in her tummy right this very moment." Madge hunched forward as if in defeat. She sat back down beside me as Eloise went on to tell us about rolling up rags and putting them in your underpants to catch the blood. "Then you rinse them out at night in a bucket of ammonia bleach," she said. She looked from me to Madge. Her smug, pimpled face showed how pleased she was with herself for bringing all of this to our attention, even though we were only nine years old, and years away from The Curse.

I stared at the water spiders as they glided across the water. The mystery of their weightlessness could not keep my attention that day. I wondered if my mother knew about this curse. She must, I thought, she'd had babies. But I'd never seen a bucket of bloodied rags in our house. I figured she must be dried up, like Eloise said.

That's why she never has any kisses or kindness—they were all dried up, just like her blood.

"Oh, and I almost forgot the most important thing," said Eloise. "And this is really important for you, Helen, in case you ever go back to the lumbering woods with your daddy. Never go in the woods for a walk or a picnic or anything when you've got The Curse. The smell of the blood attracts bears." She told us about a girl who was eaten up by a bear right in front of her entire family while they were on a picnic.

"Cookies," Mrs. Parsons sang out, coming around the edge of the pond with a tray in her hand. "I brought out a blanket so you could have a little picnic in the sunshine."

"I need to find the toilet," Eloise told her mother.

"Yes dear, you poor thing." Mrs. Parsons led Eloise away.

The Smell of Hay

Summer 1925

She said it was a game. I was never sure it wasn't. All I knew was that I was scared. Not like the feelings I had when I delivered night lunch and had to walk in the woods in the dark. This was different. It was immediate and real. I can still remember holding my hand to my heart and how it hammered in my chest. I remember wanting my father to come for me, to rescue me. It didn't feel like a game.

Madge and I were playing outside, gathering daisies and flowers to make chains for our hair. It was a warm sunny day, with a light breeze and big fluffy white clouds in the sky. We had been outside for over an hour, lost in time as we often were. Before I realized it, we had strayed far from the house and were just beside the old barn behind it. I had never been to the barn before. There were no animals on Madge's property, and nobody would have used the barn for anything I knew of.

I was picking wildflowers and enjoying the warm sunshine. I heard what I thought was a car door in the distance. I looked up, but I was on the far side of the barn and could not see Madge or the road. Just as I opened my mouth to call for her, a hand clamped down over my mouth. Madge whispered in my ear, "Shh, we have to hide." She grabbed my hand and led me inside the barn. She could see the confusion on my face. "We have to hide in here, Helen." She threw her daisies to the ground.

The barn was dark and dirty. There was an old broken-down tractor in the main room and piles of lumber and rusty tools lay on the ground. She pulled me over to a corner and shoved me down to the floor with insistent whispers.

"What's going on, Madge?" I asked as she buried me under an old tarp in the hay.

"Just be quiet, Helen. Please be quiet." I could not see her face, but her voice was shaking. I could hear her footsteps as she moved a little farther away, and then the sound of another tarp rustling. I figured she too was hiding under a tarp. In no time at all the barn door opened with a slow, creaking noise. I could make out only the shuffling of some hay on the floor. My heart was pounding and my mouth was dry. I itched from the hay and was desperate to move, but I was too scared.

As I lay there, my heart feeling as if it would come out of my chest, the edge of the tarp started to move. I could not see anything but could feel it moving away from my leg. I reached down to pull it back and something wet touched my hand. I knew immediately it was a dog. I pushed his snout away and quietly told him to go. As I was pushing his wet furry nose, I could feel something else. Fingers moved slowly down my hand and onto my arm. My heart froze and I wanted to scream, but I could not make a sound. I couldn't move, couldn't breathe, couldn't scream. Just then, the tarp was pulled away and Madge pulled me up from the ground.

"Found you!" she said.

"Madge, you scared me to death!" I screamed, shocking even myself with the tone of my voice. This was the first time I had ever been mad at her. Tears filled my eyes. She still had me by the hand, and in my other hand I was clutching the daisies.

"Oh good, Helen." She took the daisies from me. "You still have the flowers, now we can make our daisy chains." She let go of my hand and walked toward the barn door. "I guess hide-and-seek really isn't your game," she said as she walked away.

As I followed her back to the house, I could see Madge's father arguing with a boy down at the far end of the drive. The door to the boy's old truck was open and Mr. Somers stood just beside it, yelling at him. The black dog from the barn ran down the drive and jumped in the open door right before the boy slammed it shut, just missing the dog's white tail. The dust swirled around Mr. Somers as the truck disappeared down the lane. He emerged through the cloud of dust, walking toward us with a look of anger on his face I had never seen before. Madge took my hand once again and led me to the back door of the house, where we could escape up to her room to play with our flowers.

New Year's Snow

Winter 1926

I t was New Year's day. My father and Russell arrived at our door early in the morning. Snow had just begun to fall, and I was watching it through the window when I saw them appear on the doorstep. "Daddy!" I ran to him and he gathered me up in his arms, even though I was getting much too big for such things.

"Here's my girl," he roared, shaking the snowflakes from his hat onto my cheeks. Russell stood quietly beside him. His boyish looks had disappeared, and he now looked like a man of the woods. His beard was dark and curly, and he had grown thick with muscles. My father was dressed in his town clothes and they both carried rucksacks.

"You must be hungry," my mother said, giving Russell a little squeeze on the arm. She was pleased to have her son back in the house but flustered by their surprise visit. She retreated to the kitchen to prepare something. Eunie and I showed them both our readers and demonstrated how well we were doing in school.

My father beamed with pride. "I knew you were made for learning," he said.

After Father and Russell had eaten, my mother broke the silence. "Well, what is it?" she said. She sat stiff and erect. Her lips were pressed together in a hard, thin line. Eunie and I stood beside the table watching the three of them. Russell kept his eyes on his empty plate, my mother glared at my father, and my father smiled at me and Eunie.

"Russell and I are off to the United States," he said.

My mother's head dropped, her chin almost resting on her chest. She stared at her worn, cracked hands, folded in her lap. "God help me," she whispered.

"There's plenty of jobs in Boston for hard workers. We'll be going down to cut ice," Father continued, ignoring my mother's words. "We've already got a man willing to hire us and we're taking the boat out of Halifax tomorrow morning. I'll be sending for you all as soon as I make enough money for your fare."

"What about the lumbering? Has something happened?" My mother locked eyes with my father. "Are you running again?"

My father's fist hit the table and we all jumped. "Lumbering isn't working out," he said, giving her a long, hard stare. "This will be better." His voice was low and calm. I knew from his intense look that she was to accept this and question him no further. She knew it too. She stood slowly and put her hand to Russell's cheek, touching the remnants of a nasty bruise. He pushed her hand away.

"I'll be glad to be going," Russell said. "Glad for new surroundings."

I knew this was bad. There would be no surprise visits from Boston. I tried to smile back at my father, but my lips began to quiver. I went to him and wrapped my tiny arms around his big, strong neck. I did not want him to go, and I did not want to go to Boston either. Even if he asked me to come, I could not leave Madge.

"There, there now. You'll be coming to see me in no time. You and Eunie best be good helpers for your mother and keep up your school work. You'll show those Yanks just how smart you are when you come down to Boston." He lifted my chin with his giant hand and looked me in the eyes. "Who's my girl?" he whispered. I tried my best to smile back at him.

Eunie looked confused. She went to my mother and leaned into her side, stroking my mother's dress, as she often did.

Russell rose quickly, his chair scraping the floor as he stood in awkward silence. Clearing his throat, he said his stiff goodbyes and was out the door before my mother could say a word. She stood quickly and went to follow him. "Let him go," Father said, putting his hand on her shoulder. "The boy needs a fresh start. It will be good for him, good for everyone." She stared at the door and her eyes began to glisten. He gently took her hand, pulling it away from her neck where she was rubbing her scar. She suddenly turned and faced my father.

"Don't you be letting him go to pubs and drink away his life. He's still a boy and needs to be given a good example." Her voice shook with a fear I had never heard in her before.

"The boy will be fine." He handed my mother a packet with money and papers. "I'll write as soon as we are settled," he said. The door opened and closed, and he was gone.

I ran to the front window and watched as he and Russell disappeared into the whirling white. I stayed there for hours, staring into the snow, hoping they might return.

They never did.

Cracker Jacks & Nickels

Summer 1926

My mother had little faith we would be seeing money in the mail. "We're on our own now, and you best get used to it." She looked at both Eunie and I as she spoke, but I felt her words were meant solely for me.

She got herself a real job, sewing at the textile mill in town. It was hard to meet a family who did not know someone who worked at Stanfield's. They made underwear for people all over the country and hundreds of people worked there. Our neighbour, Mr. Woods, worked as a mechanic at the mill and he gave my mother a drive every morning. "Mr. Woods is a widower," my mother explained. "He's doing me a great favour." On the weekends she baked pies and bread for him as payment for driving her, and I delivered them to him.

Each morning my mother and Mr. Woods drove by Madge, Eunie, and me as we walked to school. Mr. Woods always honked the horn. Eunie would rub her eyes as they passed, watching them slowly disappear day after day. With my mother now at work, I had to be home after school with Eunie. I missed going to Madge's house, but she came to our house sometimes. She was allowed to stay until four o'clock, because she had to be home and cleaned up by the time her father got home for supper at five. I liked to play and act silly at Madge's, eating cookies and being doted on by Mrs. Parsons. But at my house, Madge thought it was fun to clean, take down the laundry, and sweep. Some days we even peeled potatoes and started supper for my mother. I suppose for Madge this was like playing house, but for me, it was work.

My mother returned from her days at the mill with a deep fatigue that seemed to drag her down, body and soul. She had little interest in our days and even less in our tomorrows. Our main interactions involved her coupon book. Each worker in the mill was paid according to how much work they did. My mother sewed the waistband, and she received a little piece of paper, a coupon, for each bundle of waistbands she sewed. Each night, she brought home her coupons and I pasted them into her book. On payday, each worker handed in their coupon book and was paid according to how many coupons they had. My mother said some girls gossiped all day and didn't get near as many coupons as she did. She told us she was one of the hardest workers and always had the most coupons on payday.

I kept busy with my school work. I loved every minute of it. Reading about different places in Canada and around the world, learning my numbers and practicing my writing—I just couldn't get enough. Every scrap of knowledge was precious to me. For the first time I had something of my very own, and no one could take it away from me. Miss MacMillan was kind and said I learned quickly and was always a great help to other students. "You would make a wonderful teacher yourself, Helen," she said one day. My heart fluttered. That was my dream, to be a teacher. Madge was the only person I had shared this with, but I thought about it all the time. To have my own teacher say such a thing was like placing a glowing candle deep inside my belly. It was a warm secret that only I knew about, which made it all the more special.

When spring arrived and summer was blooming all around us, Eunie and I brought home our school reports. For the first time, my mother truly surprised me. "Your teacher writes that you have top marks in your class," she said. "I'm proud of you, Helen. I think you've earned yourself a trip to the picture shows." In my excitement I forgot myself and threw my arms around her large, soft middle. At first she stood still, then she put her hand lightly on my shoulder.

"Time for chores," she said, and the moment was over. When I parted from my mother, Eunie stood looking lost in the corner. She still held her marks in her hand but knew there was no point in giving them over now. She was not a good student and would receive no praise today. I could not help but feel a small triumph.

I had never been to the pictures before. Madge told me about the many pictures she saw with her mother. I listened to her recall the entire story, bit by bit, the images playing in my head almost as if I were there. Now I was going to see them for myself.

The next morning was Saturday. Mother said we would be going to town and see the show after Aunt Gertie came to stay with Eunie. Even though Eunie had not received high marks, I thought she would be coming with us. But mother made a comment about the pictures not always being appropriate for younger girls and no more was said about it.

Mother complained about the heat as we started our walk to town. I found it lovely. "What picture will we see?" I asked.

"Whatever they're showing," she said. She walked slowly and clutched her purse under her arm. I was surprised at how nice she looked. She wore her best shoes and nicest dress. My mother never wore makeup, not like Aunt Gertie, but today she did have on a bit of lipstick. It was quite a walk to town, just over an hour, but I did not mind. I could walk all day to see the pictures. Just as we passed the schoolhouse, I heard the familiar honk of Mr. Woods's car.

"Would you ladies like a lift?" he said, pulling up beside us. "Not sure where you're headed, but I'm on my way to town." I looked at my mother. She smiled at Mr. Woods. A big smile. Even bigger than the kind Aunt Gertie got.

"Well, that would be wonderful, thank you." My mother slid into the front seat and I climbed in the back. "We're on our way to the pictures," she said.

"Well, this is a coincidence," he said. "I'm heading to the pictures myself. I like to go every Saturday."

From the back seat I stared at Mr. Woods's hairy neck. Dandruff gathered on the collar and shoulders of his wrinkled shirt. His thin black hair was greasy and in need of combing. I was used to looking at his face when I delivered his bread and pies. He had a long, thin nose and blue eyes that bulged beneath his thick glasses. We had never really spoken to each other before. I always knocked, he opened the door, I passed him the basket of baking, he said thank you, I smiled, and then I turned to leave. As I watched the small drops of sweat slide down his neck, I decided I liked his front view better.

The back seat of the car was covered with old newspapers. I was wedged between them, my feet resting on a stack of papers and my knees almost to my shoulders. The smell of ink filled my nose and made me think of my father. How he loved to read the paper. Mr. Woods's window was open slightly.

"Do you mind if I roll my window down?" my mother asked. "It is such a warm day."

The minute she started to turn the handle, air rushed into the back seat and the papers started to flutter, some of them flying about. I put my hands down on the stacks closest to me. I stopped most of them from taking flight, but the flapping noise continued. My mother was busy telling Mr. Woods all about my marks in school, and how the teacher had put me at the top of the class. How she was so proud of me and wasn't I just the best student. He nodded and listened politely. I had never seen her so talkative, but the wind tunnelling through the windows and the flapping papers made too much noise for me to hear everything.

I was relieved when Mr. Woods pulled up to the theatre. He let us out and went to park his car. "We'll have to ask Mr. Woods to sit with us now," Mother said. "He did drive us. It's the polite thing to do." I shrugged my shoulders and turned to look at the posters. I didn't really want to share my day with greasy old Mr. Woods, but I was so thrilled to be at the pictures that nothing was going to dampen my day.

I was allowed to pick out a treat and I chose Cracker Jacks. I had never had them, but Madge told me she ate them every time she went to the pictures. Then I saw the poster for *The Big Parade*.

There was a man who looked like a soldier and a country lady with a red kerchief on her head. My entire body tingled with excitement.

The three of us moved toward the centre of the theatre. I went to sit in the aisle seat, to the right of my mother. But she took my arm and firmly placed me in the seat to her left, between her and Mr. Woods. After the lights went down and the music started, she leaned over and whispered, "Helen, the man in front of you is so tall. Let's switch seats so you can see better."

"I'm fine, thank you," I said, not wanting to miss a moment of the show. But again, she grabbed my arm, and moved me into her seat while she shuffled over next to Mr. Woods. I didn't care where I sat. I could not take my eyes off the screen. The theatre was dark and quiet. A rich, handsome boy was going away to be in the army, leaving behind his loving girlfriend. Soldiers were fighting a war and many were being wounded and killed.

I held my breath, hoping Jim would not be injured as they walked through the foreign land where he met Melisande, the beautiful girl who could not speak English. The tightness in my stomach and the aching in my heart seemed to rise and fall with the music as the drama unfolded. Even though there were no words spoken, only those written on the screen, I was absolutely enthralled by the story. It transported me to an entirely new world. Far from Truro. Far from the woods. Far from everything.

When the lights came back on, I was stunned to find the time had passed so quickly. I was jolted back into the reality of the small theatre and the local townspeople sitting around us. That such lives were being led somewhere, and that such love existed, was overwhelming.

"Helen, time to go." Mother was already standing in the aisle. I still held my box of Cracker Jacks. I had been so taken with the movie I had forgotten to open them.

On the drive home, Mr. Woods and my mother talked about the mill and the people they worked with. I was still in Europe with Jim and his beautiful French girl. I couldn't believe one story could make me feel so sad and so happy at the same time. I thought about the horrible images of the war, the heartbreaking farewell scene when Jim left, how I laughed when he taught her to chew gum, and the beautiful reunion when he came back to find his love again. I had been so worried Melisande would not love Jim anymore because he lost his leg in the war. Was there really that kind of love out there in the world? I wanted to rush back and watch it again. I wondered if Madge had seen it yet, and I couldn't wait to talk to her about it.

Mr. Woods stopped in front of our house. He got out of the car to open the door for my mother. After I climbed out of the back seat, he took my hand and placed a nickel in my palm. "Congratulations on your school work, Helen. This is for you. Your father would be very proud of you," he said. I looked at my mother. Her smile disappeared.

"Thank you for the drive." She turned quickly and went inside the house. I had a sudden dislike for Mr. Woods and I wasn't quite sure why. But I knew I didn't like him talking about my father, and I had a feeling my mother didn't like it either. He stood with a confused look on his face. I closed my fist around the coin.

"Thank you," I said. I followed my mother inside, clutching my box of Cracker Jacks. I lay on my bed eating them one by one, still thinking about Melisande and Jim. Madge was right, Cracker Jacks were delicious.

After our day at the pictures, my mother never asked me to deliver Mr. Woods's baking again. She did it herself. We did not go to the theatre again and Mr. Woods stopped honking at us in the mornings when he and my mother drove to work. I shoved his nickel into a knot hole in the floorboards under my bed and vowed never to touch it again.

River Rocks &
Birthdays

The summers meant more time to spend with Madge. As long as I looked after Eunie and had my chores done, I was allowed to meet Madge and go down to the river where kids swam and played along the rocky shore. The river was cut between two high embankments and you had to climb down a steep path to reach the swimming hole. I could not swim, so I never went in the water. Madge was a wonderful swimmer. She could swing from the rope that hung off an old gnarly tree on the edge of the river bend. She was brave and wild, swimming with the other kids and beating every boy in every race.

The last day I ever went down to the river was August eighth, Eunie's birthday. She was turning seven years old. It was one of those sweltering summer days when the sun shows no mercy and the air is thick with humidity. Mother told us she was bringing home a little surprise for Eunie. She said we could go to the river but were to be back before she came home from work. And, we were not to swim.

"Don't go past your knees, Eunie," she said. "Make sure you watch her, Helen."

"I will." I handed her the lunch pail as she walked out the door.

Eunie and I met Madge just before lunch and we all walked down to the river. There were more kids there that day than ever before. Madge took off immediately and was swimming across the river before Eunie and I made it down the bank. I took Eunie to our regular spot where we sat on a large flat rock. Its hard, smooth surface was warm against the back of our legs and our feet rested in the cool water below. The heat hung in the air like a choking, invisible fog. There was no breeze and Eunie complained about the heat.

"I'm seven now and I should be able to swim," she said, gazing out at the other kids in the river. She rubbed her eyes and blinked quickly as she watched them splashing and diving under the water.

"You know you're not allowed past your knees, Eunie," I said. "Mama says—"

Before I could finish, Eunie jumped off the rock. The water was up to her waist and she looked proud of herself to be in so deep. "My birthday wish is to learn to swim," she said. She splashed water at me and almost lost her footing.

"You get out of there right now!" I said. "You're not allowed in that deep and I'll be the one to get in trouble." I jumped off the rock and pulled her back up.

I looked up and saw Madge talking with an older boy. He seemed familiar but I did not know who he was. He held her arm as he talked to her and she was trying to pull away. She looked angry. When his friends came over, he shoved her away. She went over to the edge of the river and sat by herself. "Stay here," I said to Eunie. I walked over to Madge and asked who the boy was.

"That's my brother," she said.

"Really?" I asked, vaguely remembering Aunt Gertie mentioning Mrs. Somers's son.

She nodded. "He's only my half-brother. My mother was married before and her husband went out for cigarettes and never came home. Then she married my father, but he doesn't like my father, so he lives with our uncle at the gas station. He's fifteen."

Madge looked down at the pebbles beneath her feet the entire time she spoke. She kept picking up little rocks and tossing them in the water.

"Do you like him, your brother?" I asked.

Just as she was about to answer, I heard a girl scream and saw people running down the river's edge. My heart froze. *Eunie!* I turned and ran up the rocky shore. She was floating face down in the water, her blond hair fanned out around her head. Her arms and legs spread wide. An older boy swimming near her pulled her from the water and turned her over. She was as limp as her doll. Her face was the colour of ash and there were foamy white bubbles around her nose and her tiny blue lips. I started to shake and fell to my knees beside her. The boy was pounding her back and I was screaming her name.

Other kids were gathering around. "She's dead!" they kept saying. "She's dead!" Some of the little kids were crying and I was holding Eunie's hand and screaming her name, over and over. The boy gave her one more whack on her back and water came pouring out of her nose and mouth. Her eyes fluttered and she started to cough.

"She's okay," he yelled. "She's okay."

Some of the older kids patted him on the back and told him good job. Eunie started to throw up more water.

"Let it out," he said. "Let it all out. Are you her sister?" he asked. I was sobbing and couldn't even see through my tears. I nodded. I could hardly breathe. I just cried and cried. Eunie was now sitting beside me.

"It's all right, Helen." She took my hand and squeezed it. "I won't tell Mama, I promise. Please don't cry."

The boy told me to take her home. I was still gasping for breath and trying to stop crying. I helped Eunie get up and we slowly walked back up the bank. I didn't know where Madge was and for the first time, I didn't care. At the top of the bank, I looked back down and saw the boy who'd saved Eunie. In all the confusion I hadn't looked at his face. It was Madge's brother. He turned and started to walk down the side of the riverbank. A black dog trailed behind him, its white tail swinging. It was the dog from the barn.

I can't remember what Eunie's birthday surprise was, but Mother never found out about our day at the river. Eunie kept her promise.

Postage Stamps
& Ammonia Bleach

Spring 1927

My father's letters were unpredictable, in both frequency and content. Sometimes he sent my mother money and a short note, and other times he wrote long letters to Eunie and I, telling us about life in Boston. Eunie preferred for me to read them out loud to her and my mother. After the first read, nobody seemed to care about the letters. Except me. I read them over and over until the paper was weak and thin. I told my mother I was saving the stamps for a collection, but it was the words I treasured. My father's warmth came right off the page. He was able to draw me into his arms and show me Boston as if I were standing right next to him.

He went into great detail about the neighbourhood where he and Russell had rented a room on the top floor of a brown house. It was an area where many people from Ireland came to make new lives in America, he said. He told us his sister Nettie and her husband helped them find their place, and his landlady was from County Cork, where his own grandmother had been born. Aunt Gertie had mentioned Aunt Nettie a few times but I didn't know much about her. He also told us Russell was quite taken with a young lady who lived close by. From the sour look on my mother's face I could tell she didn't like the sound of Mary O'Conner of South Boston, who had red curly hair, a faint Irish accent, and attended secretarial school three nights a week. I imagined Uncle Johnny would think she sounded wonderful.

He told us that cutting ice was hard work, but not much harder than lumbering. In the seasons when the ice couldn't be cut, they worked delivering it to wealthy families and grand hotels all over the city, where kitchens full of workers prepared meals for hundreds of people a day, fancy meals with five different courses, and three different people to wait on each table. In the summer, ice was kept in large warehouses, packed inside great mounds of sawdust so it wouldn't melt. He read in the newspaper about a new type of icebox which did not need ice. It was run by electricity. My father wondered if this would slow down his line of work. But he figured the poor people would always need ice, so they would have plenty of work in Boston for years to come. He told us about the base-ball games people flocked to and the many different people who crowded the city, their accents, their languages, and their unusual ways. In March, he and Russell watched the Saint Patrick's Day Parade, where thousands of people crowded the streets, drinking and celebrating Ireland.

I shared these letters with Madge, and we dreamed of moving to Boston together when we finished school. By the age of eleven, our world was a mere dot on the globe. Studying the maps of the world in school and learning about the many places outside our little county was exciting but cruel. We wanted to experience something new, not just imagine it.

A late snowstorm that April forced Miss MacMillan to send us home from school early. Madge, Eunie, and I huddled together, pushing our way through the blowing snow. It was falling so heavy that when Madge turned down her road, she was out of sight in seconds. We had on light coats and my feet were numb. In anticipation of rainy days, my mother would stuff our old boots with newspaper to help keep our feet dry. She had not predicted this storm, so we were not prepared. As we approached our back porch, Aunt Gertie opened the door and threw a bucket of water into the yard. The snow turned bright red where the water landed.

"What are you girls doing home so early?" Aunt Gertie said from the top step. Her hair was a mess, going every which way, her dress wrinkled and stained with water, and she wore no makeup or jewelry.

"We were sent home because of the snowstorm," I said. She remained on the step, blocking the door. We stared up at her. Finally, she shook her head as if to clear the cobwebs.

"Come in the house and get warm," she said. "Your mother's home from work sick and I've come to look after you."

Inside, Mr. Woods sat alone at the kitchen table, staring into a cup. I looked to Aunt Gertie.

"Mr. Woods drove your mother home, 'cause she's not feeling so well. He's just on his way home. Isn't that right, Mr. Woods?" She took his hat from the coat hook and handed it to him. He rose slowly and held his hat to his chest. He never raised his eyes or spoke one word as he slid past us on his way out the door.

Eunie threw off her coat and ran toward the hallway. "Mama!" she yelled.

"Get back here!" Aunt Gertie slammed the empty bucket on the kitchen counter. Eunie jumped and froze still. "Your mother is sick and you girls are to let her rest. She can't be disturbed." Eunie's eyes brimmed with tears. Aunt Gertie's tone shocked both of us. I knew then that my mother must be very sick. "Now, now. I didn't mean to scare you." Aunt Gertie pulled us both in for a big hug. She smelled like rose perfume and ammonia bleach. "Don't you worry about your mother. She'll be fine. But we need to let her rest for a day or two until she gets over her troubles."

For the next two days Aunt Gertie treated us like little princesses. The snowstorm continued and we stayed home from school, eating cookies and playing games together. My mother never left her room. When we asked about her, we were told she had stomach trouble and needed to rest. Aunt Gertie was continually washing sheets and emptying the chamber pot. Although she tried to keep me distracted, I could see the sheets were stained with blood, and the wash water was always pink when she threw it in the snow. Despite the wonderful time I was having with Aunt Gertie, I worried that my mother was dying, bleeding to death in her bed while we quietly played downstairs. I thought about Mrs. Parsons's daughter, Eloise, and everything she'd told us about The Curse. I didn't realize it could be this bad. She never said you could die from it. I wondered what would happen to Eunie and me if my mother died. Would we go home with Aunt Gertie? Would my father come home? Would I be able to live with Madge?

On the third day, Uncle Johnny arrived with the mail. "There's a letter here, Collie." He handed Aunt Gertie the letter and they exchanged a solemn look.

"It's from Daddy!" I recognized his writing on the envelope. "Can I read it?"

"This is addressed to your mother," Aunt Gertie said as she climbed the stairs to my mother's room. Two hours passed and Aunt Gertie still had not come back down. I was desperate to read the letter. Uncle Johnny played checkers with us. We must have played forty games that day. He smoked his pipe and laughed every time he lost. Finally, I heard the creak of the floorboards and I ran to meet Aunt Gertie at the bottom of the stairs. My mother stood on the bottom step. She was pale and gaunt.

"Are you better?" I asked.

"Your father's sent for us." She handed me the letter. "We're going to Boston."

Eunie ran around the corner and wrapped her arms around my mother's waist. They walked into the kitchen together. I sat on the bottom step with the letter in my hand. Aunt Gertie came down and sat beside me.

"Growing up can be hard," she whispered in my ear, putting her arm around my shoulder. "But all will be well, love, you'll see. All will be well."

We sat there together for some time. I stared down at the blue postage stamps on the envelope and wondered how I could tell Madge I was leaving for Boston without her.

Elevators &
Envelopes

My mother did not return to work after the letter arrived. She told us we would be leaving for Boston at the end of May. Because she was absent from work, she'd missed payday and still had a book of coupons to turn in. That Friday, she told me I was to miss school and walk to town to collect her wages. She pinned a cloth purse to my dress.

"I have a letter in here and my coupon book," she said, watching my eyes trail down to the purse. She put her hand under my chin and jerked my head up so she could look me in the eye. "Never you mind what's in there. That's not your concern. You go to the mill office and give it to the lady behind the desk. She will give you my pay. Understand?"

I nodded. I was to ask the lady to put the pay in the cloth purse and pin it to my dress again, then I was to come straight home, no dilly-dallying. Any curiosity I had about the letter was crushed by the intensity in my mother's eyes. I would do as I was told.

I knew where the mill was. It was the biggest building in town. Solid red brick, lined with windows, and with large white letters painted on the side announcing it to all those crossing the bridge into town: *STANFIELD'S WOOLLENS*.

I had never walked to town by myself. It was a cold, rainy day and I set off with Eunie. Just after I dropped her off at school, Mr. Woods drove by. There was no honk and no offer of a drive.

As I came closer to town, I realized you really did notice more things when you walked. There were large fancy houses set back from the road, peaking from behind the trees. One store had ladies' hats on display in the window and I saw people sitting at the counter in a small diner. I knew there must be a bakery nearby as the smell of fresh bread made my stomach growl.

I was sopping wet by the time I arrived at the the mill entrance. There were so many doors, I was unsure where to go. A lady walking through the large gates asked if I needed help.

"I'm supposed to go to the office and get my mother's wages," I said.

"Who's your mother, honey?" she said, bending down to look me in the eyes. I could tell she was kind by her smiling eyes, the way they twinkled just like my father's.

"Blanche McNutt."

"Oh, I know Blanche. You come with me and I'll take you to the pay office."

She took my hand and led me through a side door marked *Woollens*. We went down a narrow corridor and entered a tiny room, almost like a closet.

"Morning, Joe," she said to the man standing in the corner. He nodded and pulled a large rope. A wooden cage came down and trapped us inside the room. Then the floor began to shake. I gripped her hand and held my breath.

"Don't be scared, honey," she said, laughing, "this is just an elevator." When we reached another floor, Joe pulled the rope again and the cage door raised. We stepped into the largest room I had ever seen. There were rows and rows of sewing machines with tubes and wires connecting them to the ceiling. Beside each machine, large wooden spools of thread were neatly stacked, and at the end of the rows stood wooden trolleys full of fabric. It smelled like wool socks and my nose itched. Large fans loomed above us, blowing dust and air around the room as dozens of ladies made their way to the machines, ready to begin the day's work. From the giant windows lining the walls, you could see across the river and down the marsh for miles.

The nice lady led me to an older woman sitting at an elevated desk in the middle of the room. "This is Blanche's girl," she told the woman.

"Is that so?" She gave me a quick examination, from my ragged old boots to my sopping wet hat.

"I'm just going to run her down to the pay office so she can gather Blanche's pay," the nice lady said as she took her coat off.

"I hear your mother has got herself sick," the older woman barked down at me.

"She's feeling much better now, thank you," I said, hoping my mother didn't have to work for this old battleaxe. The nice lady pulled my hand and led me away from the workers and down another long hallway.

The office ladies gave me a glass of milk and a biscuit and told me to have a seat while they looked into my mother's pay. They read the letter and whispered to one another. Some of them looked over and smiled at me, while a couple of others shook their heads and gave me a sad nod. All at once, my chair felt like it was vibrating and the air filled with a low, buzzing sound. I looked around but could not see a reason for the noise or the vibrations.

"That's just the sewing machines, honey," said one of the office ladies. "All the girls have started their work, and the machines make quite a racket, don't they?" I nodded and gripped the chair. A door opened and I was surprised to see Mr. Woods shuffling past the office ladies, his head down. As he reached my chair, he paused for a second. I looked up and met his eyes. They were sad. He opened his mouth and I thought he was going to say something, but he simply let out a small sigh and kept walking.

A few minutes later, a man in a suit like Madge's father wore came out of the same door. He shook my hand and told me he was Mr. Stanfield. He asked that I give my mother a letter, which he handed me. "Tell your mother she will be missed," he said.

"Thank you" was all I could think to say. The office ladies showed me the way out and I started my walk home. I had the cloth envelope pinned to my dress, inside my jacket with my mother's wages and the letter from Mr. Stanfield. The rain had stopped and the sun was starting to make its way through the clouds. I walked slowly and took my time looking in the shop windows, where I saw everything from dustpans and buckets to silver candlesticks and men's shoes. There were more people out walking now, ladies dressed up for shopping and young mothers pushing baby carriages. A train passed through town and I heard its whistle as it moved slowly behind the buildings in the distance. I wondered if Boston would seem much bigger than Truro. From Father's letters I knew it would, but I felt so small that day I could not imagine any place bigger than this town.

When I arrived home, my mother examined the contents of the cloth envelope and read the letter. When she finished, she held the letter in the air and shook it before my face. "Who gave you this?"

"Mr. Stanfield," I said.

"Mr. Stanfield himself handed you this letter?"

"Yes." She read the letter again and I wondered what I had done wrong.

"Well, I'll be," she said, more to herself than me. "Will wonders never cease. They've given me a reference and a parting sum to help me start my new life in Boston." She smiled and shook her head as she set out cookies and milk.

I ate my cookies and pictured Mr. Woods's sad face that morning. I knew better than to mention seeing him.

After breakfast the next day my mother said I could go to Madge's. The snow from the storm had melted and the ground was now soft and wet with the promise of spring. When I reached the end of Madge's lane, I saw a robin hopping across the lawn. My father always told me the first robin of spring brought good luck. As I ran to find Madge and tell her about the robin, I heard a door bang shut in the distance. I looked up behind the house to the barn. Madge was running down the path, her hair flying wildly as she raced through the muddy field.

Just as she reached the lawn, I could see the barn door open again and the boy from the river come out, Madge's brother. Madge was out of breath when she came to my side. "I'm so glad you're here, Helen." She pulled me toward the house.

"Is that your brother?" I asked. "I thought he didn't come to your house."

"He only comes when Father's away. He's gone on a fishing trip." She pulled me upstairs to her room and shut the door before her brother reached the house. "We'll stay in here."

"Your ribbon has come loose," I said.

She looked into the mirror over her dressing table and smoothed down her hair, pulling the ribbon free. She stared at herself in the mirror like she was searching for something.

"Do you want me to brush your hair?" I asked.

"No." She tied the ribbon as she sat beside me on the floor.

"It's very pretty," I said, reaching out to touch the violet satin ribbon. "Is it new?" She nodded and stared at the bedroom door.

"I'm moving away to Boston to be with my father," I said. Madge kept staring at the door. "We leave next month."

Tears welled in Madge's eyes, but she did not stop looking at the closed door. "Nothing will be the same," she said. "Why can't we just grow up and go away together? We don't need to get married and have babies. Why can't we just live together and be happy?" Madge turned to me for an answer.

"Maybe you can come visit me."

"Father wouldn't let me," Madge said. She took the ribbon from her hair and handed it to me. "You take this, Helen. I want you to keep it."

"Thank you," I said. I put the ribbon in my dress pocket. Mrs. Somers knocked on the door.

"Madge," she said, opening the door, "it's time to go. Helen, I'm sorry but Madge can't play today, we have a visit planned with our friends."

On my way out the door, I could see Madge's brother sitting on the porch swing smoking a cigarette. He didn't turn my way. He just kept staring into the fields as I passed him.

When I got home, I took the ribbon from my pocket and wrapped it around my fingers. It was soft and pretty. I owned nothing like it. Mother was busy baking in the kitchen. I quietly went to her room and propped the mirror up on her dresser. I tied the ribbon around my hair as I had seen Madge do. It wouldn't stay in place and slid beneath my wiry curls.

"You'll never be like her."

My mother stood behind me in the doorway. I could see her in the mirror. "You'll never be good enough for them," she said. "She's in God's pocket, that Madge. And you and I, well, we'll never be there. Everything will always go her way, you just wait and see." Our eyes met in the round glass and we held each other's stare. "Get to the laundry." She turned and went back down the stairs.

I looked at myself as Madge had earlier that morning, searching for something but unsure what that something was. I took the ribbon from my hair and put it back in my pocket. I thought of the mean old battleaxe from the mill, looking me over like I was trash, and Madge's mother saying they were visiting friends. I felt the satin ribbon in my pocket and I hated my mother for saying such things. *Maybe Boston will be better*, I thought with a sudden longing for my father.

I went down the stairs slowly, one long step at a time. I knew the washtub was waiting for me and I was in no hurry to get there.

Green Velvet & Goodbyes

I thought we would go by boat to Boston, as my father had, but my mother said she hated boats and we would be taking the train. Eunie was excited about the upcoming trip and leaving school early. I was what my father would call *on the fence*. I was excited one minute, eager to see Boston and Father, and sad the next minute, dreading change and knowing I would miss my only friend. I had not seen Madge much in the last weeks. Mr. Somers's new interest in fishing allowed Mrs. Somers to have her son and daughter together most weekends. That meant I was not welcome in their plans.

On my last day at school Miss MacMillan took me aside. "You're such a wonderful student, Helen, and a special girl. I can't wait to see you in a classroom of your own someday." She put a beautiful, brand new book in my hand. I had never seen anything like it. Each page had a different country. A small map and flag appeared beside the text. She hugged me close and I wanted to tell her how much I liked her and that I would miss her. The words wouldn't come out. I thanked her shyly and walked home clutching the book to my chest with Madge and Eunie beside me.

Madge was quiet as we walked. Mrs. Somers was waiting at the end of their road. When we reached her, she gave me a hug. "I wanted to say goodbye, Helen." She handed me a small parcel. "You and Eunie can both use this," she said, giving Eunie a smile. "Go ahead and open it." The pretty silver wrapping paper reflected the sun. I handed Eunie my new book, pulled off the tiny white bow, and carefully unwrapped the paper. It was a box of pink writing paper and envelopes. "Now you girls can stay in touch," she said.

I thought about the many letters my father had written me. How he had painted such a vivid picture of his life in Boston on scraps of old butcher paper. I had never seen such beautiful paper as this. I imagined the delicate sheets filled with my words and Madge holding them in her hands. I swallowed a lump in my throat. "Thank you, Mrs. Somers," I said.

Her smile was just as sad as her eyes. "You're welcome, dear."

I turned and gave Madge a hug. "Goodbye, Madge." She put her arms around me and softly said goodbye. I knew those would be her only words. I could tell she was trying her best not to cry. "I'll write, I promise," I whispered. I stood and watched Madge and her mother walk away. They were beginning to look more and more alike, and from a distance they seemed like twins as they sauntered down the lane. I watched until they reached the curve in the road. Then, they disappeared.

Aunt Gertie was at the house when we arrived home. "Now that you girls are world travellers, you need to look the part." She held up two new dresses. Eunie's was a pale blue with white lace around the collar. "It matches your eyes," Aunt Gertie said, pulling Eunie in for a hug. "And you," she said, handing me my dress, "need something suitable for a young lady."

It was emerald green with pearl buttons down the front. I had never owned anything like it before. It was too pretty to wear. My eyes started to water and I buried myself in Aunt Gertie's warm embrace. "Thank you," I said.

"I'm going to miss you girls." She let the tears fall down her cheeks, messing up her perfectly made-up face.

Early the next morning I ran to Madge's house for one last goodbye. Aunt Gertie was picking us up at nine o'clock, so I thought I had plenty of time. As I approached Madge's road, a pickup truck came racing around the corner, heading back toward town. I thought it looked like Madge's brother driving, but I wasn't sure. When I was almost to Madge's house, I could hear voices down by the pond. I could see Madge and her father sitting on the stone bench. I felt like I was intruding being there so early in the morning, so I didn't go any farther. I crouched behind a bush and watched them. Madge was still in her nightgown. Her hair was tousled and her feet were bare. Her father was dressed in what looked like fishing gear, with a checkered woollen jacket, a cap, and rubber boots. Madge was crying and her father was holding her, stroking her hair and telling her she was his special girl.

"Daddy would never let anything bad ever happen to you, Madge," he said. Madge nodded her head and wiped her tears away. I knew I shouldn't be watching but I couldn't seem to move. After they left the bench and made their way to the house, I walked back out the lane and down the road. My dress had some mud from where I had knelt behind the bushes. I knew my mother would be upset with me over the dress, but I didn't care; I didn't get a chance to say my final goodbye to Madge and something about that morning left me feeling worried for her. I couldn't quite understand what it was, but it was there.

I could see everyone standing around the car as I came down the road. My mother looked furious. "We'll be late for the train, all because of you." She grabbed my arm and shoved me into the back seat of Uncle Johnny's car. "Where have you been?"

"I'm sorry." I tucked my dress behind my legs and kept my head down. We drove in silence the entire way to town. Even Aunt Gertie was quiet.

The station was full of activity. The air felt electric, and a constant buzz floated about as people raced in all directions. Aunt Gertie was watching me. She knew something was wrong. She could see the mud stain lining the bottom of my new dress. She took me aside and whispered in my ear, "Did something happen this morning, love?"

All the emotions from the past week and that morning were

suddenly too much for me to handle. The tears started to well in my eyes. Aunt Gertie took me in her arms.

"I didn't get a chance to say goodbye to Madge this morning," I said, choking back tears. "I wanted to show her my new dress. But I think she was having some kind of fight with her father, or brother. I'm not sure." I took a deep breath and tried to stop crying. "I don't understand," I sobbed. "But it just—it made me worried and now I'm so confused. I don't know if I'm scared to go to Boston or scared to leave Madge behind."

"Now, now, don't cry, love." She wiped the tears from my eyes. "You'll be all right and so will Madge. Everyone has a fight now and then. You never know what lives others lead behind their doors. Rich or poor, misery is free. My mother always said, if we all threw our troubles in a pile and were given the choice to pick out whichever ones we wanted, we would always choose our own." She gave me a smile and gently pushed me away. Holding my shoulders firm, her kind eyes searched my own. "You're a survivor, Helen. You'll see. Whatever comes your way, you'll be fine." She placed a finger under my chin. "Chin up, now," she said, and sent me toward the train.

I turned to find my mother and Eunie waiting for me. That's when I got my first close-up view of the black, steaming beast that was to reunite me with my father. I had seen trains before, but always at a distance. The noise of the rumbling engines and the blowing steam, the smells of smoke and fuel in the air, combined with the shocking size of the engine, both thrilled and frightened me. I felt we should not be so close to this iron monster that sent vibrations through the ground and up my legs.

Yet, here we were, climbing aboard and making our way into what seemed to be the belly of the beast. To my surprise, it was a different world inside, calm and much quieter. People looked relaxed and comfortable as they settled into their seats, the hustle and bustle outside the windows now something they had escaped. We were shown to our seats by a man dressed in a smart jacket with shining silver buttons running in two lines down his front. Our chairs were a rich burgundy, comfortable and plush. They reminded me of the furniture in Madge's house. I looked over to see Eunie running her hands along the soft upholstery. I knew she had never seen anything so luxurious. The train whistle blew and the beast started to creep along the track. I sat next to the window and watched Truro slowly disappear as we headed out of town. The marsh and the giant brick mill faded from view with every second.

City Sounds
& Silver Treasure

E unie and I pressed our faces to the train window, marvelling at the size of this city we would soon call home. I looked up to my mother. She was watching us with a faint smile. I took this as a good sign.

I scanned the crowds as soon as we got off the train. I knew my father would stand a head above most men, but I couldn't see him. My stomach ached. It felt like the giant wheels from the train were still chugging inside me as I jumped nervously from one spot to another to get a better view. I wondered what it would be like to have him in our lives again, to have him give me a hug and call me his girl.

It was unbelievable to me that so many people could be in the same place at the same time. There were workers, well dressed ladies, poor children begging, families hugging, people kissing, men in suits ordering other men to pick up crates and trunks. Through them all I searched for my father. A tall woman approached my mother. "Nice to see you again, Blanche," she said, giving my mother a little hug.

My mother stood stiff. She forced a smile and nodded her recognition. *This must be Aunt Nettie,* I thought. Aunt Gertie had told us all about her sister, Nettie, and how lucky we were to be able to stay with her. Aunt Gertie said she had a "heart of gold" and no children of her own, so she would be thrilled to be having us so close. She also told us her husband, Pat, was Irish, just like Johhny. "I guess us McNutt girls have a taste for the Irish," she'd laughed.

"And I have heard so much about the two of you," she said, cupping my face in her hands and kissing me in the centre of my forehead. Then she did the same to Eunie, who stood next to Mother, biting her fingernails and looking at the ground. "I'm your aunt Nettie," she said. Her smile was wide and genuine and she had the same twinkle in her eye as my father. Her hair was dark and wiry, just like mine. I liked her immediately.

Her husband, Pat, stood to the side. "Jim had to work today," he said. He must have seen the disappointment on my face. He came forward and bent down to put an arm around my shoulder. "He and Russell are full out these days, but don't worry my little lovey, you'll see them tonight." He gathered our bags and urged us toward the busy street.

"It's not a far walk to the butcher shop," he said as we walked along the sidewalk, my mother and Aunt Nettie trailing silently behind us. I ignored the large buildings and noisy traffic of the city and instead studied the crowds for any sign of my father, just in case he was coming home early to surprise me. It seemed in no time at all we had reached our new home and Uncle Pat was still talking.

"This is not the only butcher shop. This is a big city and there's a butcher in every neighbourhood. I'm a dime a dozen here." He laughed and took us upstairs to the apartment where he and Aunt Nettie lived. "This was my father's shop. I've worked here since I was a young lad. When he passed on, I took it over. I met this young beauty one day when she came in." He winked at Aunt Nettie, and you could see he still thought she was beautiful.

"That was over twenty years ago," she said as she reached for Uncle Pat's hand. "I was just a young girl from the country."

They smiled at each other and it reminded me of Aunt Gertie and Uncle Johnny. Aunt Nettie made tea and we all settled around their little table.

"The apartment across the hall has been vacant a few months now," Aunt Nettie said. "Pat's mother just passed away. Jim's moved his things in, and you can all stay there. It's got two bedrooms and its own bathroom. Russell is staying in a boarding house three blocks over." She pointed out the window as if we might see Russell walking around the corner. "It's closer to his girl." She paused and gave my mother a small grin with this bit of information. Then she turned her attention to Eunie and me. "We're so excited to have you girls here. There's a school just around the corner and lots of kids to play with. You're going to like it here, I'm sure."

My mother sat at the kitchen table. She held her cup of tea in mid-air. She took all of this information in silently. I looked around the kitchen. It was shiny and clean. The sun came through the large windows and filled the entire room with light. My mother's silence was the loudest thing in the room. I stood behind her and waited for her reaction to all this news.

"Thank you for the tea." She set her full cup down on the table, picked up her purse and suitcase, and walked to the door. "These girls are exhausted and we need to get settled." With that, she walked out the door and across the hall. My sister and I followed her, leaving Aunt Nettie and Uncle Pat sitting at the kitchen table.

Eunie and I each had our own little beds, side by side, in the smaller bedroom. The other bedroom had one large bed for my parents. We had our own indoor bathroom, just like at Madge's house. I went from room to room. I looked at every chair, the sofa, the beds, the bathtub, and wondered if Pat's mother had died in the apartment, and if so, where. Mother unpacked our things and we helped put away the few belongings we had.

Father was still not home after supper. Mother told us to go to bed. I lay in my new room listening to the strange noises outside. Cars, horns, people yelling to one another, children still running in the streets. City sounds. So many people and so much noise, yet it was the loneliest night I could remember.

I woke in the morning and for the first few seconds I did not know where I was. Eunie slept soundly in the bed just two feet away. I slowly remembered the train, Aunt Nettie, Boston, my father. *Daddy!* I jumped from the bed and ran out to the kitchen.

"There's my girl!" My father sat, smoking a cigarette and drinking his coffee. I stood for a moment looking at him. It was as if no time had passed. I could see my mother out of the corner of my eye, standing at the kitchen sink. He opened his arms and I climbed onto his knee and wrapped my arms around his neck. I breathed him in and was filled with the familiar comfort of tobacco and soap. He hugged me tight and my heart let go. Something inside me gave way and I couldn't hold it in any longer. Two years' worth of tears came spilling from me and I couldn't stop them. "It's okay," he said, hugging me tighter. "It's okay now."

When I finally stopped, he set me on the floor in front of him, his hands on my shoulders. "Look at the pretty young lady we have here." He looked over at my mother. "I think she has grown two feet since I left Nova Scotia."

"They both keep growing," Mother said. She set a plate of eggs and bacon in front of him. "They both need new shoes."

My father ate his breakfast slowly, watching me. He couldn't seem to stop smiling and his eyes were as bright as I'd ever seen them. "We'll get you new shoes," he said, winking at me. "But first, I have something for you." He took a little box out of his pocket and handed it to me. The box was navy blue satin. I ran my fingers over the silky fabric, then opened the lid. Inside was a small silver pin in the shape of the letter *H*.

"It's beautiful," I said. My fingers traced its curves. I hugged him again and whispered my thanks. Mother watched but did not say anything. I wondered if she was given a pin too, but I didn't ask. Eunie came in then, rubbing her eyes. It was her turn to receive a hug and a present. But she clung to my mother's skirt and held out a shy hand to receive her new set of paper dolls. She said a quiet thank you.

"She doesn't remember you as well," my mother said.

"Let's see what time Frank has." My father handed the familiar watch over to me. I held the warm metal in my hand as I had so many times before. Grinning at him, I pushed the button and told him the time. "Just like the old days." He stood and put the watch back in his pocket.

My mother handed him his lunch as he headed out the door. "Off to work," he said. He disappeared, not to be seen for the next two days.

Baked Beans
& Biscuits

A t the end of our first week in Boston, I learned why it was nick-named Bean Town. Aunt Nettie threw a party with a great feast to celebrate our arrival. I can still taste the molasses in those beans. She was an amazing cook, and we were not used to such a delicious meal. Dark sweet beans, golden salty ham, and light fluffy biscuits smothered in butter. *Little clouds*, Uncle Pat called them. "They just melt in your mouth," he said.

"The best cook we know," my father said to Nettie as she gave him his second heaping plate. My mother barely touched her food and didn't utter a word. Russell and his sweetheart, Mary, arrived just after we sat down to dinner. She was a pretty girl and her cheeks flushed red every time someone spoke to her. I loved her Irish accent. It was more musical than Uncle Pat's. Aunt Nettie made a big fuss about getting them dinner and sat them next to my mother. I had never thought about how my mother must have missed Russell, her only son. I could now see it on her face as she watched him with pride. Her worries had been for nothing. He had made his way in Boston and had not been sucked into a life of drinking as she had feared. He spoke softly as he answered my mother's questions, but he did not elaborate or ask anything of her and was shy with Eunie and me. He was a stranger to me now, a grown man in another country, living his own life. He kept fidgeting in his seat and looking at the door. After the meal, Russell stood at the table and put his hand on Mary's shoulder.

"We've got news." He looked down at the table. "We're getting married."

Aunt Nettie was the first to jump from her chair and rush over to hug them both. "Congratulations!" she said.

Russell's face was now as red as Mary's. My father and Uncle Pat slapped him on the back. "Well done, well done," they said.

My mother remained seated. Her quiet presence filled the room and made little space for any jubilation. Her voice broke through like the crack of an axe. "I assume this will be soon then, this wedding." She looked from Russell to Mary, letting her eyes travel down to rest on Mary's lap.

"We hope to be married next month." Russell put his arm around Mary and led her from the table.

"I understand," my mother said. She shook her head slowly as she stood. She left the table and walked out the door, back to our apartment.

"I think she's just surprised," Aunt Nettie said, resting her hands on Mary's shoulders. "She's been through a lot of changes this week." She went to the cupboard and brought out a bottle of whiskey. "Let's toast the couple." Soon, my mother's lingering dark cloud dissipated as they poured drinks, talked about weddings, and compared the beautiful churches throughout Boston.

It was over a week before any mention was made of Russell and Mary again. I had just come inside from the street when I heard my mother and Aunt Nettie in our apartment. I knew they hadn't heard me come in. The door had been open just an inch and I had been so surprised to hear my aunt Nettie's voice so agitated I had not yet shut it.

"We all have our pasts, Blanche, as you well know. I remember when you came to Boston all those years ago. Think of that and don't be so quick to judge Russell's girl."

"That wasn't the same and you know it." My mother spoke so quietly I was on tiptoe, straining to hear.

"Russell loves that girl, and that should be enough, Blanche. You really need to get off your high horse." Aunt Nettie's voice dropped.

"I just had a letter from my old friend Connie Larkin. You remember her, Blanche? She still works at the mill. She wondered if you ran to Boston every time you got yourself in trouble."

I heard my mother stomp into her room and slam the door with such force the pictures on the wall shifted. When Aunt Nettie turned the corner into the living room, she saw me at the door. I stood completely still as she placed her hand on my cheek and gave me her kind smile. She reached past me and closed the door with a flourish.

"Look who's home," she said, raising her voice. "Come in, Helen."

She patted my shoulder softly as she walked out, back to her apartment. I was at a complete loss as to what I had just heard, but I was grateful my mother was in her room and I would not have to look her in the eye just yet.

The Pledge of Allegiance

Fall 1927

I pledge allegiance to the Flag of the United States of America, and to the Republic for which it stands, one Nation under God, indivisible, with liberty and justice for all.

My relationship with Boston was complicated. It was a mixture of the unknown and the familiar. I found it hard to adjust to the constant cars, noisy streets, and crowds of people. Even though I had lost Madge, I had my father again. I felt safe. It felt like home.

Life soon settled into a routine, as it often does. Mother stayed home most of the time with Eunie close by her side. I was given the rare gift of freedom. I spent my time exploring the neighbourhood. There were children everywhere. Playing in the streets, down the alleys, and on the front steps of the many buildings that housed our neighbours. It took some time to shed my shyness and join in the games, but once I did, I was one of the gang. They laughed at my accent and said if I didn't open my mouth, I would surely pass for just another Irish kid on the block. "You've the freckles for it!" they said.

Aunt Nettie often took me with her to run errands. "So you can get the lay of the land," she said. We rode the trolleys and I had to laugh at myself for wondering if Boston would be anything like Truro. This place was unlike anything I could have dreamed. The noise never stopped. The cars, the trolleys, the crowds, they all had a humming rhythm that was the life of the city. If a silence were to come over Boston, I was sure I could blink and see nothing but fields of green. The city went on forever. You could surely walk for hours and hours in any direction and it would never end. Brick building after brick building—stores, restaurants, butcher shops, bakeries, churches, factories, hospitals and, houses—it just went on and on. And the people looked different, too. I couldn't quite understand what it was that made them different; their dress, the way they walked, the way they smelled, or the way they ignored each other. They were simply different; they were city people.

I liked to see if I could spot any young girls that looked like they may be in a new country, too, unsure of what may become of them. I never saw any. I did see many young girls dressed in pretty dresses with shiny new shoes and perfectly curled blond hair, and they made me miss Madge.

A man put his hand on Aunt Nettie's backside while we were on a crowded trolley early one morning. She quickly grabbed my arm and we moved away. We got off at the next stop and ended up walking six blocks. She warned me then about strange men.

"This is a big city with lots of characters, Helen," she said. "You need to be careful. There's lots of dirty old men out there looking for young girls just like you." I wondered what dirty old men truly looked like. The man on the trolley was clean-shaven and wore a suit and tie. I thought of Madge's father, and the fine suits he always wore.

I wrote to Madge the day after the incident on the trolley. I told her all about the city, our apartment, Russell's engagement, and my aunt Nettie. I told her I would be starting school the next week and how excited I was. I told her I missed her and hoped she'd had a fun summer. Aunt Nettie took me to mail the letter. "It's to my best friend, Madge," I said as we walked the two blocks to the post office.

"She must be very special to be chosen as your best friend," Aunt Nettie said.

"She is." I didn't tell her Madge was my only friend.

My Boston school was in no way like my old school. The sprawling brick building had three floors and indoor bathrooms. There were hundreds of kids and they weren't really that different from the kids at home, except for their accents and the way they dressed. Even the poorest of them seemed to have a decent set of clothes, and no child here arrived at school without shoes. I was happy to recognize many from playing games in our neighbourhood streets.

On the first day, my mother walked with Eunie and me to ensure we were properly registered and placed in the correct classes. She told the administration lady that I was top of my class in Nova Scotia.

"Is that so?" she replied, a cigarette hanging from the corner of her mouth. She wrote my name in a black ledger. "Let's just wait and see how she does here." She stopped writing and looked up to give me a quick once-over. "This isn't Canada."

And with those words of encouragement, I began grade six on the second floor of the Washington Branch Middle School. My teacher was Miss Duggan. She was a large, lumbering woman with long grey braided hair. She did not look like a teacher to me. But I was soon proven wrong. She informed us she had been teaching for thirty years and it was her mission to prepare us for the next level of our education. Her class was full of rules. I didn't mind, I was happy to be back at school and learning new things. Eunie and I walked to school and home again together, but rarely saw each other during the days.

It wasn't long after we started school that Eunie's teacher sent a note home saying Eunie needed glasses. She was constantly rubbing her eyes, it noted, and could not see the blackboard properly. Mother paced back and forth for hours waiting for father that night. When he finally came through the door, smelling of liquor, they had a huge fight about money. In the end, I don't know where my mother found the money, but Eunie soon had glasses. Her eye-rubbing was replaced by the new habit of constantly pushing the small gold rims back up her little nose. It was hard to say if they helped her sight, but it didn't help her marks, and she continued to hate school. As always, she was happiest at home with our mother.

I found the hardest thing to get used to at our new school was the ceremony every morning where we all put our hands on our hearts and recited the Pledge of Allegiance. I was used to singing "God Save the King" and it took me a few days before I got the words of this new ritual right. I liked the line "one nation indivisible," and I tried to think of it as one *family* indivisible. I was plagued with worries about my family. Could we all stay together here forever? Would my father stop drinking? Would my mother stop being angry? Would there come a day when my father simply would not return?

As I said the Pledge of Allegiance, it became a kind of morning prayer for me. For my family. Could we ever be indivisible?

In the meantime I kept sending Madge letters, one every two weeks. She never wrote back.

Irish Lullabies
& the Smell of Books

Mary Margaret Sullivan was my first friend in Boston. She had eight brothers and sisters and they all had two names, just like her. Frances Marie, John Ryan, Patrick Doyle, and the list went on and on. It was hard to keep them straight and it was impossible to figure out who was who, but it was definitely fun trying. Mary Margaret and I went to different schools. She was taught by the nuns at a school around the corner from mine.

"They're a mean lot, Helen, the nuns," Mary Margaret told me. "I can't wait to be done with it. I hate every minute."

Even though we didn't go to church, my mother said I was a Baptist. "You'll not be taught by the likes of those nuns," she told me when we first arrived in Boston.

I was fine with that. I loved my school. I excelled at my studies and was a member of the school Literary Club. Every Wednesday after school we met at the big library two blocks from Aunt Nettie's house. The first time I walked into that library my jaw must have hit the marble floor. I had never seen such a place. So many books. And the smell. I had not realized that books had a smell. I stood with my eyes closed, taking in long, deep breaths. Mr. McDade, my English teacher, read my mind as he watched me that first day. "Smells like learning, doesn't it, Helen?" I smiled and nodded in agreement, sure that I could actually smell the words in the air.

Mr. McDade was unlike any teacher I had ever met. He took pleasure in everything our class did together. He would give us a

book to read and then choose a question to match the main char-
acter or the book's theme. We would then be tasked with writing a
list to match his question. At first, I thought they were very strange
exercises. We certainly didn't do this kind of thing back home with
Miss MacMillan. The first list we did was *What makes you nervous?*
I made two lists, one for myself and one for school. My private list
contained loud silences, promises, the wrong side of a door, and
empty whiskey bottles. The list I gave Mr. McDade was similar to
the other students': big spiders, thunder, and moving to new places.
At the last minute I added one from my private list to Mr. McDade's:
promises. Mr. McDade circled that one word, *promises*, and returned
the paper to me. "This is what I'm looking for," he said.

Mary Margaret had no such interests. She laughed and shook
her head when I told her about Literary Club. "You'll be a teacher
yourself one day, Helen, if you keep this up." I just laughed with
her. Little did she know, her worst nightmare was still my dream.

On my first trip to Mary Margaret's house, six-year-old Connor
James Sullivan seized me by the arm as soon as I took my first step
up the front stairs. "Mary Margaret told us you were coming," he
said. "What kind of a name is McNutt?"

"I'm not sure," I said.

He stared at me with his intense little eyes. He held my arm tight.
"You're not Italian, are you?" He looked over to Mary Margaret
and opened his eyes wide with fear.

"No, I'm from Canada."

He looked relieved. "That's good."

He pulled me up the stairs to meet the many other Sullivans,
who all spoke at once and made more noise than my entire Nova
Scotia school at recess. When they weren't talking, they were laughing, hooting, hollering, fighting, teasing, and eating. I sat silent, my
mouth gaping as I looked from one person to another. They lived
on the third floor. There was a family on the first floor, a family on
the second, and the Sullivans on the third. Connor James told me
the first floor were Sullivans too, but not related.

"My da says you can't swing a cat in this neighbourhood without hitting a Sullivan." Connor James swung his arm above his head like he was about to launch a cat through the window. "We're the best ones, though." He winked and gave me a smile.

At first, I could not understand how they all fit in such a small space, but I quickly realized it really did suit them. The children were always sitting on one another's knees, rolling around wrestling or in some other entanglement, which made them seem like less of a crowd. Mary Margaret showed me the room where the children all piled into two beds and slept together, sometimes four to a bed. You could tell they wouldn't have it any other way. I thought about the times Eunie and I slept in the same bed and again felt a familiar sense of loss, of something missing between us.

When Mary Margaret first introduced me to her mother, I thought she may be an older sister, not the mother of so many children. "So, this is Helen, the Canadian who loves books and school," said Mrs. Sullivan. She shook her head and looked around the room at the gaggle of children. "God love you, child, you'll have to do your best to fit in with this ignorant lot. Not one of them likes school. But I'm holding out for my little Shannon." She took the baby in her arms and gently handed her to me. All the children gathered around to look at her sleeping in the arms of the Canadian girl. The room was quiet for the first time since I'd entered.

"What's her other name?" I whispered, fearing I would wake her.

Mrs. Sullivan laughed and tucked Shannon's blanket around her little ears. "She's only got the one for now. She's only three weeks old. She's named after a river where I grew up in Ireland."

"Isn't she just the most beautiful little lass you ever saw?" Mary Margaret was at my side.

"She is," I said. It was the first time I'd held a baby, and I was in awe. She had jet-black hair and tiny fingers. Her round, rosy lips moved as she slept. She was perfect. I watched her peaceful face and thought about Russell and the beautiful baby he would have had. They'd lost theirs just a month after Mary's belly started to show.

"Can you believe someone left this here, Helen?" The children slowly stepped away and I saw Mrs. Sullivan sitting at a piano in the corner. "It was here when we moved in. Mr. Sullivan says it was a gift from the angels, sent to the Sullivan family." They all remained quiet as their mother's voice filled the room with an Irish lullaby. Little Shannon continued to sleep in my arms as her mother's fingers danced lightly across the keys. Her voice was soft and soothing, rising and falling effortlessly like the birds from the woods at home. As I watched the children silently stare at their mother, each one entranced by the lullaby, I fell in love with the Sullivan family.

Mary Margaret's mother made me feel like part of their family from that day on. Not only was I encouraged to learn the piano, sing Irish songs, and change baby Shannon's nappies, I was encouraged to eat. Mrs. Sullivan's food was a new experience. Savoury beef stew and warm sodabread smothered in butter. Everything she made was delicious and everything she did was wrapped in kindness. There was always something simmering on the stove, someone eating at the table, someone yelling at somebody else, someone getting a hug, and someone laughing. It all went round and round in a circle of family love. They were a source of constant astonishment.

Mary Margaret, on the other hand, could not get used to the quiet of Aunt Nettie's house. "Don't get me wrong, Helen," she said one Saturday, "I like it here, you can actually hear yourself think, but the constant quiet makes me a bit nervous, like I'm waiting for something to happen."

After a trip to the pictures one summer afternoon, Mary Margaret and I came back to my house. Aunt Nettie was helping Uncle Pat in the shop. "Your mother's gone shopping, Helen. Why don't you girls go up to my place and help yourselves to some cookies and milk. I just baked them this morning," she said.

We were about to go back outside when Mary Margaret knocked her glass of milk onto the floor.

"I'll get a rag," I said and went to the hall closet. When I came back, Mary Margaret was standing in front of the kitchen cabinet holding a framed photograph in her hand.

"Who's this?" She held up the frame. "He looks like you, Helen. Is this your da?"

I took the frame and stared down at the young couple. My mother held a small bouquet of flowers and my father wore a suit, his large hands hidden in his pants' pockets. They both stared at the camera, stiff and serious.

"It looks like a wedding day photo." Mary Margaret took it back from me. "Although she's not wearing a proper wedding dress." She looked around the room and then lowered her voice. "I was looking for something to wipe up the milk and I found it under the tablecloths in this drawer."

"We'd better put it back." I took the photo from her and buried it under the tablecloths.

"Is that your parents?" Mary Margaret's voice was now just a whisper. "That picture was taken in front of this building, Helen, right down on the steps of the butcher shop."

I nodded and closed the drawer.

Ice Skates

Summer 1928

"This isn't working out, Helen." Those were her words. I'll never forget them. She spoke like it was some kind of equation from my mathematics class that she couldn't quite grasp. My mother looked past me to an unknown point of interest on the wall. She refused to meet my eyes.

"I'm returning home and Eunie's coming with me. We don't have enough money to bring you." She paused, then added in a more hushed tone, "Not just yet. When I can save enough to bring you home, I will send it to your aunt Nettie and she'll arrange it."

That was my mother. No preamble, no sentiment or discussion, just the hard facts. And with that, she walked into her room and then reappeared with her suitcase in one hand and Eunie in the other.

"I bought you a new dress for the start of school next week. It's in your room. Remember to obey your aunt Nettie and do your school work." She made her way down the narrow stairwell toward the front door. Eunie twisted around, adjusted her glasses, and gave me a last wave goodbye. She did not look as surprised as I must have. She wore her best dress, whereas I was in my usual play clothes waiting for the neighbourhood kids to start a game outside. I lifted my hand, a silent gesture for Eunie just as the door shut, and they disappeared.

I stared at the sun filtering in through the window of the front door. I wondered where my father had been these past three weeks, if I would ever see him again. Dust floated in the shafts of light and I was reminded of God's lights from the logging camp. I had not seen them in many years, and their wonderment and beauty had almost faded from my memory. That seemed so long ago, another life really. Another country, another little girl, another time. I watched the light until Aunt Nettie came and suggested I have a rest, as this was quite a lot to take in for such a young girl.

I lay on my little bed hugging my knees to my chest. I was more shocked than upset. I knew my mother could be heartless, but to leave me behind was a new level of cruelty. Tears slowly slid down my face as I pictured my mother and Eunie boarding the train. I stared at the large scab on my knee and started to pick it. As I pulled the dry, dead skin away, the pain distracted me briefly and my tears stopped. I kept at it, picking it away bit by bit. I was reciting the Pledge of Allegiance silently in my head, over and over again—*one nation indivisible*—as I revealed the fresh pink flesh under my scab. When it started to bleed, I wiped the blood away with my thumb and brought it to my lips. My last memory of that day is the bitter taste of blood that lingered in my mouth.

Like many other children, I adapted to my circumstance. I had no other option than to accept it. Life went on. I went to school, I turned thirteen, I played with my friends, and sometimes I was lucky enough to see my father. One of my most memorable visits was on a cold Saturday in January. I was at the kitchen table doing my school work when Father arrived at our door. His visits were always a welcome surprise. I never knew when he would show up or what kind of visit we would have. It could last three days, or thirty minutes. It could be full of excitement and laughter or it could be a quiet talk about school and my studies. Either way, I treasured those times. On this day he said we were going ice skating.

"I don't know how to ice skate!" I laughed and looked at Aunt Nettie for support.

She smiled, went to the hall closet, and returned with a pair of ice skates. "These should fit you," she said. "Lord knows the last time I wore them."

"It was five years ago." Uncle Pat took her in his arms and danced around the kitchen. "We skated arm in arm around the Commons like two young lovebirds."

Aunt Nettie blushed and pushed him away gently, but she couldn't get the smile off her face.

"I borrowed a pair too," my father said. "So, we're all set."

The sun was out, but the air was cool and crisp. A storm the night before had left ice on the bare branches throughout the Commons. Everything glistened. It was like the starry night sky had forgotten to leave. The pond shimmered and many people were already skating across the clear blue ice. My father helped me put my skates on and asked if I was warm enough.

"Just perfect." I took his hand and walked onto the ice. Within an hour I was gliding across the pond with ease and confidence. I was a natural and I loved it.

"I knew you would take to it," my father said as he skated beside me. It seemed strange to see him in such a setting. He looked twice the size of any man on the ice, yet he moved with grace. I asked who taught him to skate and a sad smile spread across his face.

"It was my best mate, Robert. He was the most glorious skater I ever saw." He scanned the crowd and nodded, confirming there was indeed nobody present on this pond who could skate as well as his friend. "And he was fast, too, no one could catch him. He was a country boy like me, and we use to have bridge races back when we were your age. You could only do it in the coldest weather, when the river froze solid and you could skate for miles from one bridge to the next. He always won. Nobody could touch him.

"Word of his speed got around and the townies wanted him to come in and race on the marsh. He thought it was hilarious. Him with his old blades, and them with their fancy new Starr skates. He could have had hunting knives strapped to his boots and he would've still won! The townies would make a day of it and take bets on the races. They set up courses on the large frozen marsh, just beyond the mill. And boy did they regret it, those townie boys. Bobby was in another league. They couldn't come close to him. He sometimes finished so far ahead, he would do another lap, just to show them how fast he was. He never looked more alive than when he was on the ice."

"Does he still skate?"

"No." My father dropped his chin to his chest. "He passed a long time ago. He was like a brother to me, Bobby."

I could hardly hear his last words, and with his head bent down, his hat made it impossible to see his eyes. He was quiet for a few minutes, so I stayed silent. "But," his head shot back up, "now I have a new skating partner, and I couldn't be happier." He had his old smile back and I could not help but smile too. His eyes sparkled as he took my hand and we made one last trip around the pond before heading back to Aunt Nettie's.

Russell joined us for dinner that night and I told him about our day skating at the Commons. He laughed and said he would never be caught with a pair of skates on. "I'd break my neck," he said.

"Oh, I don't know about that." My father gave Russell a smile. "I think you might surprise yourself—you could be a natural like your sister."

"Do you think I could be as good as your friend Bobby some-day?" I asked.

Aunt Nettie dropped her fork and we all looked at her. She stared at my father with a look of shock on her face.

"Who's Bobby?" Russell asked. Their heads turned in unison to look at him.

"Just an old friend, son." He patted Russell on the shoulder. "Nobody you would ever know."

My father pushed his chair back and suggested a drink. Uncle Pat got the bottle out of the cupboard and that was the end of our special day.

Bobby was not spoken of again and that was the last time my father took me skating.

Jane Eyre
& The Body of Christ

Spring 1930

The months and years passed, and life continued to surprise me as Boston felt more and more like home and Nova Scotia felt further and further away. If I wasn't with Mary Margaret at the Sullivans, I was helping Uncle Pat in his shop, studying for school, or attending Literary Club. Mr. McDade was planning a recital for the club, where we would read from a poem or book in front of our families. I was practicing a scene from my favourite book, *Jane Eyre*, every day after school and hoping my father would be able to come hear me speak.

Little Connor James was about to have his first Communion. I had no idea what this entailed, but according to Mary Margaret it was a tremendous occasion, made even more special for Connor James as his lifelong ambition was to be a priest. The church was ever-present in their lives. Twice a week the long line of Sullivans marched single file, making their pilgrimage to the Catholic church two blocks away, each child pulling at some part of their uncomfortable outfit as they dutifully trailed their mother. Mr. Sullivan was often absent from this family parade, but I didn't find that surprising. That part seemed normal to me. In addition to these biweekly expeditions, they also went to countless other holy events: confessions, baptisms, and confirmations, most of which were followed by parties full of food, music, and neighbours. This was the first time I had been invited to the party afterwards.

"Trust me, Helen," Mary Margaret said. "The party is the best part. The only part worth going to. You're lucky you don't have to suffer through the church service. I wish I could just go to the party!"

When I'd first come to Boston and told Mary Margaret I had never been to church, she immediately took me to peek through the doors of the Immaculate Conception Church on the corner of Boylston Street. I had seen the massive stone churches that seemed to appear on every corner of the city, and heard their bells ringing out on Sundays, but I had never been inside one. When she pushed opened the giant wooden doors, we stepped inside and the silence overtook me. How could anything so large, and with such immense presence, be so quiet? I stood at the back of the pews and looked around in wonder at its beauty. The sun streamed through the large stained-glass windows and the polished wood of the arched, domed ceiling was almost too high to see. It was a peaceful, welcoming place and I was filled with the same feeling I had when I first discovered the woods at the logging camp. I felt safe.

Mary Margaret broke the silence when she saw one of the priests entering what she later told me was the confessional. "We'd better get out of here quick, Helen, before Father Gallagher sees us. If Ma catches wind of me sneaking around here, she'll tan my hide for sure."

The party was on a Sunday afternoon and my recital was the following Wednesday. When I came home from school Friday, Aunt Nettie was waiting for me.

"I have a surprise for you, Helen, for the party." She took my hand and led me to the parlour, where a floral dress lay across the sofa. I recognized the material and knew what a kind gesture it was for her to make this dress.

"Thank you," I said. I took the dress and held it up against my chest. "I can wear it to the recital, too."

On Sunday morning I practiced my lines from *Jane Eyre*. I chose the passage that always made me think of Madge. I closed my eyes and said the words over and over again, hoping I would always be able to keep them in my heart and mind.

It is as if I had a string somewhere under my left ribs,
tightly and inextricably knotted to a similar string situated
in the corresponding quarter of your little frame. And if that
boisterous channel, and two hundred miles or so of land come
broad between us, I am afraid that cord of communion will be
snapt; and then I've a nervous notion I should take to bleeding
inwardly. As for you,–you'd forget me.

I opened my eyes when I heard a knock at my door. Aunt Nettie came in holding a letter. Her eyes were red and I knew she had been crying. I recognized my mother's handwriting on the envelope.

"What is it?" I jumped from my bed. "Has something happened to Aunt Gertie?"

"No, dear, everybody's fine. Everything back home is the same as always. I've had news from Blanche." She led me back to the little bed. "She's sent the money for your train ticket." She sat down beside me. "She wants you to go home." The letter rested on her thigh and as she spoke, she ran her hand over it, smoothing it out as if she were trying to erase the words within it. It reminded me of the way Aunt Gertie always smoothed out the tablecloth when she had something to say. They were very much alike, my father's two sisters.

"But I don't want to go," I said, tears welling in my eyes. "I thought this was my home now." I looked into her kind eyes, so like my father's, and I saw that my mother would get her way.

"We will be heartbroken to see you go, Helen." Her voice cracked sightly and she bent her head in resignation. "You must do as your mother wishes. And your father agrees."

I pulled away from her and was on my feet again. "He knows? When did the letter come?" My tears were quickly replaced by a sudden burst of anger and I raised my voice to her for the first time.

"How long have you all known this?"

"The letter arrived just yesterday," she said. "I went to see your father when he got off work. He said you had to obey your mother."

Obey my mother. Go back to Nova Scotia. I was in complete shock. I didn't think she would ever send for me. I thought my life was now in Boston and I dreaded the thought of leaving. I was happy. I had school, friends, and occasionally, my father. Now she was taking Boston away from me with little more warning than when she left me.

I sunk back down on the bed in defeat, and laid my face on my pillow. "I hate her," I said.

"You don't really mean that." She rubbed my back, comforting me as she had so often done over these past years. How many times had she sat with me in this very room? She'd held me and let me cry when my father didn't show up for my birthday dinner, she'd taught me how to roll rags when I finally got The Curse, just as Eloise had predicted all those years ago, and she listened to me talk endlessly about Madge and all the fun we use to have.

"I really do hate her," I said. "And I always will."

"Hate is not a simple thing, Helen." Aunt Nettie's voice was calm and quiet. "I've always believed there are two kinds of hate. Some people's hate, it's like the scorched edges of a sheet of burnt paper. It's delicate. The bits of ash and blackened char can be knocked off and wear away, and in no time you're back to a clean, fresh sheet. That hate is not long-lived. The other kind of hate is like charcoal ground into silk. It takes time to form and tends to last forever. Nothing can wash it away. In the end, it destroys whatever beauty there once was." She pulled her hand away and helped me to sit up again. "Soon, my dear, you'll once again have a clean sheet." She handed me the envelope. The money was gone, just one sheet of paper remained, my mother's sparse words scrawled across the page. Her letters had always been meagre and disappointing. This one was no exception. "No matter what you may think, your mother loves you. How could she not?"

When I arrived at the Sullivans', the party was well underway. Connor James was delighted to be the centre of attention and the children were devouring the cakes and other goodies the guests had brought. You could hardly squeeze through the living room. Mary Margaret found me and introduced me to Father O'Brien, the priest who had given Connor James his first Communion. His tiny frame was lost inside his long, flowing robes. A bony, wrinkled hand found its way out of the folds of black fabric and grasped my hand tightly. "God bless you, child," he said, then shuffled over to the table which was overflowing with loaves of homemade bread, and platters of chicken and ham. Connor James appeared at my side. We both watched the old priest make his way slowly across the room.

"We think he's one hundred and five years old," he said with a wink. He took my hand and pulled me away from Mary Margaret, who was now in a conversation with some of the first-floor Sullivans. He shut the door to one of the bedrooms. "I've got a surprise for you, Helen," he said.

"This is your day, Connor James, I should be giving you something special."

"Don't worry about that now, Helen. Today's the best day ever. I've been gathering envelopes all day. I figure I've got near three dollars in Communion money so far." He patted the pocket of his suit and smiled up at me. He looked like a miniature man in his black suit and starched white shirt. No doubt every Sullivan boy had once worn that suit to their own first Communion, but Connor James looked wonderful in it. "Patrick was an altar boy this morning and as a Communion present, he pinched me an extra piece." He pulled something out of his pocket and put it in my hand. It looked like a thin piece of dried toast.

"What is this?"

"The Eucharist," he said with a whisper, taking a quick glance around to make sure we were still alone.

"The what?" I turned it over in my hand.

"I wanted you to be part of the day too." He took it back and held it up between us. "I mean, I know you aren't Catholic, but I thought it would be okay if you took Communion today, 'cause you're just like family." He looked so sincere and his eyes pleaded with me as he spoke.

"What do I do with it?"

"Just close your eyes and stick out your tongue," he said. I could see how much this meant to him, so I did as he asked.

I felt something rest on my tongue and I automatically opened one eye slightly. Connor James's eyes were closed, his hands together in prayer. I quickly snatched the object from my tongue and closed my mouth. With the most solemn and serious tone I have ever heard come out of a child, he said, "The Body of Christ."

I closed my eyes tight. "Eat it, Helen," he said, and I pretended to chew. "You have accepted the Body of Christ." His voice had returned to its normal, squeaky tone. He watched me swallow and nodded in satisfaction. "I've no need to worry about you now, Helen, you'll always be a part of us." He paused and shook his head. "It's too bad I couldn't get any of the wine, which is really the Blood of Christ. But Patrick couldn't swing that." Connor James's little freckled face beamed with pride. He wrapped his arms around me and thanked me for coming to his party, then ran back to the other room. I tucked the Body of Christ under the sash of my dress.

I found it hard to enjoy the rest of the afternoon, knowing this may be the last time I would see these people whom I had come to care for so much. I told myself I didn't want to share my news and put a damper on the party, but deep down I knew I could never tell them. I could never face such a hard goodbye.

At the end of the day, Mrs. Sullivan wrapped a plate of food for me to take home and share with Aunt Nettie and Uncle Pat. "Just bring the plate back next time, my love." I was holding little Shannon as Mrs. Sullivan smiled at me with the same care and attention she gave all her children. Before I put Shannon down, I whispered in her ear and confessed my final farewell. I knew she wouldn't repeat my words.

"We'll see you when we see you," Mary Margaret yelled out the third-storey window as I walked down the street. That had always been her special way to say goodbye. I couldn't bring myself to turn back and yell the same thing in return, as I had done so many times. Tears crept down my cheeks as I walked forward, just me and the Body of Christ.

My father was sitting in the kitchen when I arrived home. A train ticket sat on the table. I wiped the last of my tears and set the plate down beside the letter. "I'm going to miss my girl," he said, his voice quiet. I knew there was no point in asking him to let me stay. He would always follow her will.

"When do I leave?" I asked. As I reached for the ticket, the Eucharist fell from my waist to the floor.

"What's this?" my father asked, bending down to pick it up. I quickly grabbed it and tucked it back under my sash. "Just a goodbye present from a friend," I said.

He said no more, but watched me read the ticket. I was to leave Wednesday morning. I would miss my recital. He could see the disappointment on my face.

"Could you read me your poem now?" he asked. "Aunt Nettie says you've been practising and I'd be honoured if you would say it for me here, just like you would have on Wednesday night."

"It's not a poem," I snapped, surprising myself with my tone. "It's a passage from a book called *Jane Eyre*." I went to my room and picked up the book. I held the weight of it in my hands and felt completed defeated. When I opened it, it fell to a page where I had underlined a small section. I walked back to the kitchen, stood in front of my father and read.

"Do you think I am an automaton?–a machine without feelings? and can bear to have my morsel of bread snatched from my lips, and my drop of living water dashed from my cup? Do you think, because I am poor, obscure, plain, and little, I am soulless and heartless? You think wrong!"

Floral Curtains & Foggy Mornings

I stood with the crowd, clutching my paper lunch sack and small purse. I could barely make out the approaching trains through the thick, wet fog. My dress itched and I felt out of place. The faded floral pattern was better suited as the curtains hanging from Aunt Nettie's windows than as a dress for a fourteen-year-old girl. I was lucky to have a dress, I knew that. But I did not feel lucky to be returning to my mother and life in Nova Scotia.

My father and I said our goodbyes on Monday evening. Aunt Nettie had Russell and his wife and my father for dinner. The last supper, and final farewell. I could hear the guilt in his voice as he told me it was for the best. "You should be home with your mother and sister, Helen," he said, "and someday we'll all be home in Nova Scotia together, I promise." Even though I was old enough to recognize a hollow promise, I couldn't resist the twinkle in his eye, and that smile that showed me he loved me. He wrapped his strong arms around me for one final hug and I did my best to ignore the faint smell of whiskey that lingered on his breath. Even though his visits had been rare, and even though he had not fought for me to stay, he was still everything to me. I would miss him.

Aunt Nettie and Uncle Pat took me to the train station after breakfast. "Just stay on the same train, Helen," Uncle Pat said. "Don't get off at any stops, and don't you worry about anything. Nettie wrote a note for the conductor, so he can keep an eye on you. He'll make sure you get there. Twenty-eight hours and you'll be back in Nova Scotia." He patted me on the shoulder as he spoke and nervously looked up and down the station. I nodded and tried to hold back my tears. He gave me a quick hug and stepped back to give Aunt Nettie her turn.

"Train 53, Helen. Remember that, train 53." Aunt Nettie was crying as she handed me the note.

"I'll be all right," I said putting the note in my purse. "Thank you for everything, I'm going to miss you both."

She stepped closer and held me tight. "We'll miss you, my love," she whispered in my ear. Uncle Pat took her by the arm and led her away. They disappeared into the crowd as the fog swallowed them up. I was left to find my own way.

As sad as I was to leave, it was my anger that surprised me that morning. It grew with every passing minute. It was the powerlessness of not being in charge of my own future that burned deep in my belly. I was angry at my mother, my father, and at the world for not caring about my dreams. I did not ask to return to Nova Scotia. But why should that matter? I did not ask to come to Boston in the first place. And I definitely did not ask to be left behind. It seemed strange now, but being left behind had been a blessing in many ways. I had finally been free to be me. I no longer had my mother hovering over my shoulder, questioning my whereabouts, my cleanliness, and my behaviour. Of course, Aunt Nettie looked after me and did her best to make me feel loved. But in the end, she wasn't a mother. She wasn't my mother.

For all her cruelties and punishing ways, it was still my mother's love I craved. Deep down, I knew that. Even at the age of fourteen I could feel it. That made me angry as well, to recognize there was a small part of me that was happy my mother wanted me back, that she hadn't forgotten me. The freedom of Boston could not compete with the deep pain I carried. The pain of being left behind, of being abandoned. It was like a bruise, the kind you don't even notice at first, but once you notice its darkening marks, it grows bigger and uglier by the day. And sometimes it leaves a faint reminder, a discoloured blemish of proof that it never really healed.

Someone yelled for passengers on the 53 to start boarding. I slowly made my way to my seat. The thrill I'd felt when I boarded the train years earlier on my way to Boston was gone. As the city faded from view, I thought about Mr. McDade and the recital I would miss that night. He didn't know I was leaving. I couldn't summon the courage to tell him. I hadn't told anyone, not even the Sullivans. I thought maybe I could just fade away, and they would all forget I had ever been in Boston. But I knew that wouldn't happen. I held my purse tighter, thinking of them all, knowing Connor James's Eurcharist was wrapped in a tissue inside.

Aunt Gertie met me at the train station. I knew she would. Tears spilled over her rouged cheeks as she watched me make my way through the crowd. I ran to her, put my arms around her, and held tight. Neither of us spoke for some time. I had missed her the most, and her smile told me she felt the same.

"Look at this beautiful girl." She gave me a kiss on the cheek. "You've gone and grown up on me." She wiped away her tears. "I guess that's life." She flashed her famous red-lipped smile as we made our way to the car.

We took the slight bend in the road and the little crooked house came into view. "I'm nervous," I said. "I don't know what I'll have to say to her."

"Don't you worry about any of that." Aunt Gertie reached over and squeezed my hand. "This is your family, Helen. For the good and the bad, this is it. And they love you."

Eunie stood in the doorway. She looked so different. Same hair, same smile, same old hand-me-downs, but she held herself up with a new confidence. I could see my mother behind her, peeking over her shoulder.

"You go in now," Aunt Gertie said. "It'll be all right, you'll see. I'll be back over to visit tomorrow." I took my suitcase and got out of the car. She drove away and left me standing in the swirls of dust on the edge of the road.

"Helen?" Eunie ran down the steps and gave me a hug. I was surprised by such a show of emotion, but when she stepped back and pushed her glasses back up her nose I had to smile; she hadn't changed that much.

"Don't look so shocked," my mother said. She remained on the top step. "You were missed, Helen." She turned and walked back inside the house. "Come, have something to eat. You're nothing but skin and bones."

The house remained the same. The blue walls were still faded, the floral dishes were still chipped, the white curtains still hung crooked, and the creaking furniture still creaked. Everything looked grey. Even with the sun shining in through the small window and a light breeze blowing the curtains, it felt closed-in and oppressive. The same dark clouds that had always been here hovered overhead. My mother looked grey, too. She had lost weight and her face carried years not yet lived.

"I need some air," I said and ran back outside. I couldn't even cry. My tears had all been shed in Boston. I knew I was here to stay. "I'm going to visit Madge," I called out. My voice sounded so loud on this lonely country road. My mother appeared at the door and watched me walk away. She said nothing, but I felt her old words like stones on my back as I walked down the road.

You'll never be good enough for them. You'll never be like her.

Mrs. Parsons opened the door. "Well, well, well, look who it is. Your mother's finally brought you home. Did your father come with you, Helen?"

"No, Mrs. Parsons. Is Madge home? I'd like to see her, please." Mrs. Parsons moved to the side, indicating I could enter the house.

"She's in the kitchen." She put her hand gently on my arm as I passed. "She'll be glad to see you."

I stood and watched Madge from behind. She had not heard me come in, and she sat twirling her hair with one hand and flipping the pages of a magazine with the other. She was staring out the window, not even looking at the pages.

"Hi, Madge," I almost whispered, not wanting to startle her. She slowly turned and looked at me with a blank stare. It took only a second, but I could see her glazed-over eyes brighten with recognition. A smile spread over her face and she rushed over to hug me.

"I can't believe it's really you, Helen." She stood back and spun me in a circle. "Look at you! You look so wonderful and grown up."

"Well, so do you, Madge." I smiled at her, noting her stringy dull hair and her ill-fitting dress. Her fingernails were bitten to the quick.

"Are you here to stay?" she asked.

"Looks like forever. At least until you and I can get ourselves back to Boston. You'll just love it there, Madge."

"Helen!" Mrs. Somers flew into the kitchen and wrapped her arms around me. "I heard you were coming back. How are you? How have you been?" She tightened the belt on her housecoat and flipped off her slippers as she sat on a kitchen chair. She looked much older. Her hair was not quite as blond as it once had been and her sad eyes were surrounded by dark circles, which made her look even more troubled than before.

"I'm just fine, Mrs. Somers." I was shocked at how easy it was to lie about such things.

It was a blessing when school began two months later. Miss Mac-Millan was pleased to see me, and I told her about the literary group I'd attended in Boston. It felt strange to be back in a one-room schoolhouse, but I was glad to be learning again and proud to now be studying the grade-ten courses. There were fewer children in the higher grades, especially boys. Many left to work in logging camps or on family farms. I wondered if they missed school, as I would. But I knew most boys could not wait to be rid of the confines of the classroom, to start making money and become men, just like Russell had.

Madge and I fell back into our friendship with ease. She had obviously missed me; I could tell by the way she clung to my side and hung on my every word. I never asked why she hadn't returned my letters. Maybe that just wasn't her way. I felt protective of her.

She seemed like a china doll teetering on the edge of a shelf. I didn't want her to fall.

I turned fifteen that first month of school. Madge was a fully formed woman and I could see it in the eyes of the boys and men who watched her. I was beginning to develop the curves I had so longed for but still felt like the ugly duckling next to her. She paid no attention to the boys. She not only ignored them, she seemed to hate them. I was just as happy to be with her, so I too kept my distance from the boys. Gerald Johnson was the only one who caught my eye, and he sometimes talked to me and asked for help with his school work, even though he didn't need it. Madge told me to keep clear of him, that he only wanted one thing. I didn't know about that, but I did as she said and stayed close to her instead.

In December my father arrived home. My mother showed no surprise when he walked through the door two days before Christmas with a bag of presents and a job waiting for him at a logging camp near New Glasgow. Here we all were again, a family of strangers struggling to make it work somehow. I was happy to have my father back, but not surprised when he left for weeks at a time to work at the camp. He came home some weekends. He still drank. They still fought. Time passed and stood still, all at once.

Train Whistles

Spring 1931

I t was Madge who made me go that day. "Please, Helen, do it for me," she begged, saying her brother was really sweet on me. "He talks about you all the time. He thinks you're so pretty and would love to take you skating."

I loved the idea of going skating. I'd been many times since Father took me to the Commons in Boston. But I didn't have much of a good feeling toward that boy. He was five years older than me and quiet. Too quiet. And it was hard to get a good look at his eyes. His head was always drooped, looking at something no one else seemed to see. He was certainly handsome enough, with dark blond curls that couldn't quite be tamed. I never saw anyone so tall. Even taller than my father, but not the strong type. His clothes hung off his bony shoulders and he didn't hold himself up quite right.

I did go with him that day, the day of my first kiss.

I was supposed to be tidying the house, but I disobeyed my mother and left to meet him. I don't know why I went; maybe I still felt indebted to him for saving Eunie all those years ago. He said he knew of a good pond out past the McCurdy Farm. We drove in silence down a deserted road. The stench of cigarettes and motor oil filled the truck. He must have borrowed it from his uncle who ran the garage. I sat in one spot, trying to avoid too much contact between the grimy upholstery and my favourite cream-coloured coat with the chocolate buttons. The brown tweed seat had lost that itchy fabric feeling and wore the slick sheen of dirt and age. The thin layer of grease covering the windows distorted my view of the passing fields. It looked like a winter desert, void of life. I twirled my skate laces around my fingers and kept my eyes on the passing view.

The sound of a match striking snapped my attention back to him. He took long, deep drags of his Lucky Strikes. I twirled the laces tighter and tighter, turning the tips of my fingers blue. The weather had warmed in the past two days and I worried the ice may not be safe. He assured me he had been there just yesterday, and it was still nice and thick. "A patch of glass," he said. "Too good to be true."

I had never been out with a boy before. I couldn't imagine any boy wanting to take me anywhere. I was no beauty. I hadn't grown out of my freckled face, wiry hair, and long skinny legs, like Aunt Gertie said I would. I wasn't like Madge. And at fifteen, no boy had really even interested me. Except Gerald Johnson, of course. He was shy and polite, and always held the door open for the teacher. You could tell he had real manners.

I continued to twirl my laces, looking down at the skates in my lap. The laces were different colours, both repaired with knots in several places. Running my hands along the cracked white leather and dull blades, I thought of my father. He had brought the skates home earlier that winter. In a swirl of tobacco, rum, and snow, he'd staggered through the porch door and dropped them on the kitchen table among my schoolbooks.

"For my girl," he roared and placed his large, gentle hand on my shoulder. I smiled up at his kind, worn face. His eyes twinkled and he gave me a wink, heading back to his room where he passed out with his boots still on. The skates were too big, so I stuffed the toes with newsprint and wore them with pride.

The squeaking brakes brought me back from my thoughts. Before I could ask where the pond was, he was on me. His lips crushed mine, his hands groped. The more I pushed him away, the harder he pressed. "No!" I screamed, fighting for air.

"Yes," he grunted, tearing at my coat. My voice rose to a frantic pitch. His grew deeper and more demanding. I shoved him away. He held me down. His stale breath was on my neck. His vulgar hand up my skirt. I lashed out, scratching for his eyes.

Then—it blew! Loud, long, and strong. The train whistle. The blast stopped all motion instantly. Our eyes met for the first time since I had entered the truck. He reminded me of a wild animal, his eyes a mixture of violence, lust, and fear. Mine must have shown pure panic. Stumbling out of the truck, I slipped in the melting snow and landed in the muddy slush. I started running and didn't look back. The train was only twenty feet from the truck. Boxcars rushed past me one by one in a blur of snaking metal. Their thunderous roar drowned out my pounding heart as I ran alongside them, heading home.

The next day a policeman knocked quietly on our door just after breakfast. I felt a grip of panic when I saw the officer, worrying my mother would find out about Madge's brother. "Are you Mrs. James McNutt?" the officer asked my mother in a hushed tone. Turning from him, she looked at me.

"What has your drunken father gone and done now?"

The officer took a step further into the kitchen. His shiny black boots glowed next to the faded grey linoleum.

"Your husband has been in an accident, ma'am." He placed his gloved hand on her stiff shoulder. Reading from a small notepad, his voice wavering slightly, he looked at me as he read: "'The remains of Mr. James Isaac McNutt have been recovered on the CNR tracks some 120 miles east of Truro, in the Antigonish area. Mr. McNutt was struck by the number 7 eastbound Sydney express. His body was identified, through papers found in his clothing, by Officer Ralph MacGillivray.'"

I heard it again then, tearing through me and drowning out the officer's words. The train whistle. My eyes flew to the hook in the porch. *My skates!* I must have dropped them when I ran from the truck. I let out a small whimper as tears slid down my cheeks. The officer, so clean and official in his pressed uniform, led my mother to the sofa.

"Make some tea, Helen," she said, taking her apron off, folding it, and setting it on the arm of the sofa. A widow at last.

Sewing Machines & Stockings

There wasn't one soul who wanted to know my grief. Not my mother, not my sister, not even Madge. It made them uncomfortable and it made them nervous.

I like to think they were incapable rather than unwilling. It seemed my father departed with more than my broken heart; he took the words from the mouths of those left behind. Madge was unable to look me in the eye or speak more than an "I'm sorry" when her mother brought her to pay respects at our house. Even Aunt Gertie was stricken mute by the loss of her brother. As he was lowered into the ground, she put her arm around my shoulders, and for the first time I could remember, she brought me no comfort.

"I have no words, Helen," she said. "I simply have no words."

It seemed my life was falling apart

The day we buried my father, my mother found me behind the house. The laundry was piled in buckets around my feet. "Tears won't bring him back," she said. "If they couldn't bring him back when he was alive, they certainly won't now. It's time to move on." She nudged a bucket of clothes with her foot, so that it touched my leg. "Clean your face and get to work." She opened the door and paused. "I'm going in to write Russell. Tell him about your father."

The stench from the thawing mud under my feet and the stale laundry water filled the cool spring air. I watched her go back inside as I pulled a man's undershirt from the closest bucket, once white but now grey and worn. I wondered whose father it belonged to.

From that day on, I kept it inside. Like the love I had for my father, my grief was my own. I held it like a secret. It was hard, but I became very good at it. There were questions from authorities, letters from the railroad company, and inquiries into my father's death. It seemed the accident was just that, and the small settlement the lawyer told my mother was surely her right, was not in our future. Her defeat was, once again, my problem.

"We're moving to town, Helen. And you'll be leaving school to help us make ends meet." She cleared the dinner plates and stood at the sink with her back to me.

"I love school." It was all I could think to say.

"I don't," Eunie said from her chair.

"Eunie's not old enough to work. You are." She didn't raise her voice as I thought she would. She turned and I could see how tired and worn she looked, like so many of the shirts she laundered. The fight she'd once had in her was fading away. "I'm not asking you, I'm telling you. I found you a spot at the mill. You'll do well there. You're smart, and you'll no doubt work your way to supervisor one day."

The mill! Was this to be my future? Sewing men's underwear and lining up with the ladies for my coupon books?

"This is your last week of school, Helen." She turned and went to sit in the other room, leaving the dishes for Eunie and me to finish.

Eunie sat with her head down. "I'm sorry, Helen," she whispered in a rare show of support. And that was that. Another decision made about my future. I was not to be a teacher. I was to follow my mother down the same miserable path.

I kept the truth to myself that whole week. It was hard to sit in the classroom, knowing I would soon be out in the world working. It was hard to even imagine hovering over a sewing machine all day. I still wanted to learn and I still wanted to spend time with Madge. I couldn't bear to think of her disappointed face when she learned I would soon be leaving her again. I still felt ashamed of how I'd left

Mr. McDade's class without saying goodbye. I knew I couldn't do that to Miss MacMillan. I decided to tell her on my last day of school.

When the day came, I told Madge and Eunie to walk home without me, saying I was asked to stay and speak with the teacher. When I told her the news, tears started to well in my eyes, and Miss MacMillan looked as shocked as I was at my sudden emotions. She put her arm around me and told me not to worry. "I'll speak with your mother, Helen. You are a gifted student and she'll have to understand how close you are to finishing your studies, writing your exams, and going on to the normal college. You are meant to be a teacher."

"It's okay, really it is, Miss MacMillan." I attempted a weak smile and handed her my books. "My family needs the money now."

She said no more, so I was sure that was the end of it.

I was shocked to hear Miss MacMillan's raised voice when I woke up the next morning. I came downstairs to find her face to face with my mother. They were squared off like two bulls.

"These are my wishes," my mother said. "Our family's business is none of your concern."

Miss MacMillan's face was crimson. I had never seen her so angry, not even when the Stevens brothers fought in the aisles. "She *should* be a teacher," Miss MacMillan said.

"Well, I *should've* been a lot of things, but that's not the way it went. We're moving to town and we'll be working together to feed our family. That's all I have to say." My mother turned and brushed past me as she left the room. Miss MacMillan's eyes started to well up.

"I'm sorry, Helen," she said.

"Thank you." I wrapped my arms around her.

"Don't thank me, Helen, I've done nothing but make your mother upset."

"No, I'll never forget it," I said.

She left quietly and her visit was never discussed. We moved four days later, and I started work at the mill the next Monday. I was fifteen years old.

The mill was just as I remembered it from years ago when I had gone to collect my mother's wages. I thought I might recognize some of the ladies from that day but the faces all looked the same, and now I was just another in the crowd. Some were smiling, some complaining, some laughing, and some dreaming. No matter what they were doing, they were all the same, just getting through the day the best they knew how. I spent my first day in training, learning how to stitch the seams of underwear. The constant vibration and the noise of rows upon rows of machines all humming at once was unnerving. I focused on my machine. I tried to ignore the dust itching my nose and the heat that grew by the minute, bringing sweat to the back of my neck. I knew that sewing machine was like an animal I had to tame.

"It's all in the rhythm," the ladies told me. "Don't worry about your speed for now, it's the rhythm you want to master. If you've got the rhythm of the machine, you'll do just fine."

After a few hours of fighting it, I started to feel the rhythm, how to touch the pedal just so, easing it down with my foot, making it do what I wanted. They told me I was a natural. *Just my luck*, I thought. It was a long day, and I was happy to hear the bell mark the end of my shift. My mother found me and told me she was working late, so I walked home alone.

Our new house was only a few blocks from the mill. We shared the bathroom with an older couple who lived on the first floor and a dark, narrow staircase led to our three rooms upstairs. The smell of cabbage and sausage was constantly climbing the stairs and the stench seemed to live in our clothing long after we left the building. Eunie and I were once again sharing a bed in a cramped little space behind the living room. She was just thirteen then, and expected to continue her studies in town, even though she was not a natural student.

Though there was nothing special about the house, I'll never forget it, because it is where I first met him.

When I turned the corner off Queen Street after my first day of work, I could see a group of boys sitting on the rock wall that lined the front of our property. I put my head down and walked toward them. One boy stood and blocked my way.

"Good afternoon," he said. I looked up to meet his blue eyes. He was handsome with a crooked grin and a straight nose. He could not have been much older than me. He winked. "Is it Hazel?" he said. "Or Hilda?" He saw my confusion and pointed to my pin. The *H* my father had given me. "It's Helen!" He knew by my expression he had it.

"Excuse me." I pushed my way past him.

"Certainly." He bowed dramatically as he let me pass. "You have a lovely day, Helen."

I walked up the three stone steps and then down the walkway.

"Helen?" I paused slightly but did not turn. "You may want to take a look at those stockings tonight, there is a little tear on your left leg." I kept walking, my face turning darker by the moment. When I got inside I looked at the back of my left calf, and there was the tiniest little tear in my stockings. How could he have seen that? I peeked out the window, but he was already gone. I examined the tear. I smiled at the thought of him looking at my legs.

He was there every Monday when I came home from work, always with a few other boys. If they saw my mother with me, they wondered off as soon as we turned the corner. If she wasn't with me, they stayed. His name was Edgar. He drove a truck but had Mondays off. He thought a lot of himself, I could tell that from the beginning. He wasn't someone I would've picked for myself. But he'd picked me, and that was enough.

Ivory Combs

My new life was strange and confusing. I was still a child in my mother's eyes, but she also saw me as a working woman, a co-worker who faced the same daily struggle. It wasn't spoken of, but it definitely was a struggle to get through the day, get through the week, and start again. I knew my mother was a smart woman and I imagined we both had the same feelings about working at the mill. You had to work hard, but it wasn't hard work. It required a strength beyond the physical to keep you detached enough to accept the reality of your days. Not everyone who worked there felt this way. I could see that was clear. Some openly hated it, and some were simply happy and didn't seem to give it much thought. I wasn't the only young girl there, and although it was obvious we were all "fresh," the other ladies treated us as equals in most ways. We were meant to simply pull our weight and not cause trouble.

Soon after I started, I got oil on my dress from a machine. I thought I had ruined my dress, and my disappointment was obvious. My supervisor promptly put me in my place.

"Listen here, freshy." She raised her voice for all to hear. "Start dressing like you're going to work, not like you're looking for a beau. No need to look pretty for this lot. Make yourself a sewing apron and save your fancy frocks for the dance hall." Her speech got a laugh from everyone in earshot. My cheeks turned red, and I blushed to think they thought I was capable of getting a beau or going to a dance.

My mother must have heard the exchange. She found me during lunch. "Don't worry about what they think," she said. "Most of them don't have much thought in their heads. Just do your work, you'll get on fine." It was peculiar to have this shadowy alliance with my mother and I feared it would take me farther from Madge and our plans of leaving this place.

My first pay just happened to be the week before my mother's birthday. I knew my earnings would go to her, to help with the rent and bills. So I was surprised when she gave me some money one night after dinner. "You work hard," she said, placing the money on the table. "You should have something for yourself now and then." She handed me the dishtowel and told Eunie to go finish her studies. They both went to the other room while I started the dishes.

Since we'd moved to town, I had not seen Madge once. So I was elated when she was able to come to town on my day off for some shopping. She was still in school, but I had a feeling she did not go very often and that she really had no interest in talking about it, or anything else for that matter. She hadn't looked quite herself when I'd returned from Boston, and now she hardly resembled the pretty, confident girl I once knew. The lively bounce and mischief were gone. I worried about her. "Is everything all right, Madge? You don't seem yourself today…"

"What could be wrong?" she answered as she bit her fingernails. "It's the same old me."

She had always been so careful about her appearance, but now her hair was dull and looked like she hadn't washed it in ages. Her dress was wrinkled and dirty. Her shoes were scuffed, and she wore no lipstick or makeup. When we went into the ladies' shop on Prince Street, she showed no interest in any of the new clothes or shoes they had on display. I picked up a pink dress and said it looked like it was made for her, but she just curled up her nose.

"I thought we were looking for a present for your mother," she said. "You won't find what you're looking for here."

The first thing I saw when we entered the drugstore was a display of hair combs. I picked one up and was immediately transported back to our little cabin in the woods. My mother loved to have her hair combed. It was one of my chores when I was a young child. Why I was chosen for this intimate task, I could never understand. "Get the comb, Helen," she would bellow after breakfast. Comb in hand, I appeared each morning ready for our daily ritual. I can still feel the pointy teeth in my hand as I dipped the stained ivory comb in a jar of water and then ran it through her thin, greying hair. Flakes of dandruff rose to the surface of every perfectly combed wave as the teeth traced a precise grain across her scalp. Eunie envied me this task, I knew. She sat and watched us every morning, and sometimes asked if she could try. I would have gladly given up the ivory comb to my sister, as the sight of the dirty water made me nauseous. But it would not be heard of. Mother denied Eunie's request every time. "This is Helen's chore, no discussion."

It had been many years since I had performed that ritual, and for the life of me I could not explain why I would want to bring back such memories, but I decided to buy my mother a new ivory comb for her birthday. Madge showed no interest in my purchase. It was like spending the day with a ghost; I could see her, but she wasn't really with me.

I had the comb wrapped in pink paper and put a little ribbon on the box. It was sitting on the kitchen table when she came in for breakfast the next morning. Eunie had already left for school, so it was just the two of us. My mother raised an eyebrow and gave me a small smile as she opened her present. She held the comb in her hand, said thank you, and slipped it back into the little box.

"Happy birthday," I said, handing her a cup of coffee. She nodded and took it to her room. I never saw the box or the comb again.

The next time my mother gave me money from my wages, I bought myself a lipstick and saved the rest in a tin can under my bed. I decided it was easier to be co-workers.

Rock Walls
& Bitter Chocolate

Summer 1932

A year of Mondays vanished amid playful banter and innocent teasing before Edgar asked me to the pictures.

"I want to see this boy. He'll come to the door and take you out properly," my mother said. She knew about him already. Our Monday meetings were not exactly a secret. She saw the boys hanging out in front of our steps. But she had never met Edgar, and I had no hope that she would like him. Aunt Gertie was visiting the afternoon I asked my mother about going to the pictures.

"What's his last name?" This was Aunt Gertie's first question about everybody.

"Campbell," I said.

"From up the east end? Deke Campbell's boy?" she asked.

"I don't know his father, Aunt Gertie. He doesn't talk much about his family. I know he lives up off the hill, that's all."

"Well, you be careful, they've got a reputation, those Campbells." She raised her eyebrows to my mother. They both held their teacups in mid-air and looked at me as if they were seeing me for the first time. My mother's eyes trailed down from my carefully done hair and my growing bosom to my slim legs and dainty feet.

"He's a nice boy," I said. "I've known him for over a year, Aunt Gertie. He's been nothing but nice to me." My mother held out the tea towel in response. I took it and started to dry the dishes.

The night of the pictures, Edgar arrived with a small bouquet of flowers. *He* is *handsome*, I thought as he took off his hat and smiled that crooked grin of his. I went to take the flowers, but he pulled them back out of my reach. "They're for your mother," he said with a wink. Oh, he was sly all right. I had told him enough about my mother. He knew he would have to work hard to gain her trust. He even had a small box of chocolates in his pocket for Eunie. He was a natural charmer and he knew it. In no time, my mother was gushing over him like a schoolgirl herself. I had never seen her like this. Of course, I'd never seen anyone make a fuss over my mother. It was a night of firsts all around.

I can't remember what the picture was. But I do remember the walk home. When we reached the rock wall, Edgar cupped my face in his hands and kissed me gently on the lips. It was my first real kiss. Soft, gentle, and powerful. It woke up an entire new set of senses I had not known existed. My skin tingled from my lips to my toes. His lips tasted like a mixture of tobacco, chocolate, and something else that was foreign yet familiar; it reminded me of the damp moss of the woods. The musky scent of his skin and the surprising pressure of his lips left me feeling as though I was floating right off my feet. I was dizzy when he stopped and looked down into my eyes. "I'll be seeing you again real soon," he said. And then he was gone.

I don't know how long I stood there watching him walk away; it could have been minutes, but it felt like hours. I do know that I felt like a new person when I walked through our door to my waiting mother.

It was both surprising and distressing to my mother when only a month later I had two young men vying for my attention.

Gerald Johnson, whom I'd attended school with, now lived only two streets over with his aunt and uncle. He was a couple of years older than me and was working at the bank. His uncle worked there too, up on the second floor with Madge's father. It was no surprise he had a job there; he'd been smart in school, and I knew he'd make something of himself.

Gerald often called on me Friday nights. It just so happened I never saw Edgar on Fridays, as he worked late that night. They knew about each other, but none of us ever discussed it. I tried to think of Gerald as my friend and Edgar as my boyfriend, but it wasn't always that easy. Gerald was kind and thoughtful. He asked me about my days at work. He took me out to the Palliser, the most expensive spot in town. "You deserve a treat, Helen," he'd say. "You work so hard."

Gerald sometimes dropped in to visit and would often walk me home from work if he could manage to leave the bank early. He would be waiting for me in his suit, standing outside the mill gates. Always eager, always smiling.

"He's out of your league, Helen," my mother would say. "He's not the boy for you."

But I liked him. He was shy. We did not always have much to talk about, but he liked to ask me questions about the mill and gossip. His cousin also worked there, so he knew about many of the quarrels that went on between some of the ladies—who was the best sewer, whose niece or daughter was promoted over someone more deserving, who needed to bathe more, who took too many bathroom breaks—it went on and on. He laughed at it all, and so did I.

At Christmas that year, Gerald gave me a new housecoat. "You said you found your room cold," he said when I opened it. That was Gerald.

Edgar gave me a box of chocolates. The same box he'd given my mother and Eunie on our first date. But this time they came with a kiss that left my legs weak, and that made all the difference.

I knew things couldn't continue with both Gerald and Edgar, but I didn't know what to do about it. The Valentine's dance decided it for me. Edgar asked me to go with him, and I said yes right away. But when I really think about it, he'd told me we were going to the dance together. "I'll be taking you to the dance Saturday, Helen," he said. I thought nothing of it at the time.

"Edgar asked me to go dancing Saturday, and I said yes," I told my mother. Aunt Gertie was sitting in the living room having a cup of tea and gossiping with Mother. As usual, she had some opinions.

"What's happened to the Johnson boy?" she asked, knocking the ashes from her cigarette into the clean ashtray on the side table.

Before I could answer, my mother was in front of me. "You can't string along two boys, Helen. It doesn't look good." She shook her head. "People will talk."

"I'm not stringing anyone along." I sat on the sofa beside Aunt Gertie. "I'm really not." I looked at her for a bit of support, but she could see the worry on my face. She raised her eyebrows at me. "I don't mean to," I added quietly.

"Young boys have hearts, too." Aunt Gertie spoke seriously as she took my hand. "Sometimes we can't see the result of our actions. Sometimes, especially when we're young, we're too absorbed in our own worlds to see how we affect others. You have to make a decision and choose between these two boys before someone is hurt, maybe even you."

When Gerald walked me home from work the next day, he asked me to the dance. I told him I was already going with someone else. "Do you really like this other fella, Helen? Is he good to you?" I heard the disappointment in his voice, and I couldn't look him in the eye.

"I really do like him." I stared at my shoes. I didn't know what else to say. I was desperate not to hurt Gerald's feelings.

"I hope you'll be happy," he said.

Before I could speak, he turned and walked back down the street. I was left standing in front of the rock wall, watching him go. That was the last time he came to call on me. He was such a kind boy, and it was only years later that I realized why I liked him so much. He'd reminded me of my own father, always making me feel special.

Madge and I had been seeing each other on the rare weekend that we could arrange it. She was still in school and basically miserable. I told her about Edgar, but she didn't seem to want to talk about boys. I asked her to come stay with me for the weekend and come to the dance with us. I was sure Edgar could bring a friend along for her. To my surprise, she agreed, but said she would meet us there.

We were sixteen and going to our first dance.

Sure enough, Edgar brought along one of his buddies for Madge. She was not there when we arrived, so the three of us made our way through the crowd and found a table. The hall was packed with young people. At first, I didn't think I knew anyone. But when I looked harder, I realized many girls from the mill were there. They just looked different, all made up and dressed in their finest. I had hoped to buy a new dress, but we didn't have the money for it. Now, seeing the other girls, I felt a bit self-conscious. Edgar must have read my mind. He leaned in and whispered in my ear, telling me how beautiful I looked. I stopped caring what anyone else thought at that moment. He took my hand and we turned to watch the band.

They were set up on an elevated stage at the end of the room. I had never heard a live band before, and I stood in awe as their instruments filled the room; their pulsing energy seemed to be coming right up through the old floorboards. The band was shrouded by a smoky haze, but I recognized the man playing piano from the shipping yard at the mill. There was a heavy-set guy on guitar, a skinny kid held the trumpet to his mouth, his fingers moving like lightening, and the fellow out front pressed his lips against the microphone as if he were kissing a woman. His voice rose above the crowd like magic. Couples were swinging each other back and forth across the dance floor with an energy and pace that felt contagious. I had no idea how to dance, but I couldn't wait to get out on the dance floor.

Edgar led me to my seat and continued to hold my hand as I told George all about Madge. When I felt Edgar's hand slip from mine, I turned to see he was looking toward the door. I followed his gaze, and that's when I saw her standing in the doorway. Everyone seemed to be looking at her. It was the old Madge: shimmering blond hair swept up in a wave, a fitted yellow dress showing off her figure, and a bright smile, complete with red lipstick. I ran over and gave her the hug I had been longing to give her.

"You look beautiful," I whispered in her ear.

"Mommy took me to the hairdresser." She reached up to adjust her perfect blond hair.

I could finally see a bit of that old sparkle she'd had as a young girl. She gave me a small smile and I took her to the table to meet the boys.

George Archibald may not have been the best-looking or brightest of the bunch, but that night he certainly had the attention of the room when he walked onto the dance floor with Madge on his arm. She really did turn heads. I could tell she didn't care for George, but she was polite, and the four of us spent the night dancing and talking. George was drinking from a flask, and Edgar and Madge took a few sips. She was in a feisty mood, laughing and making jokes. I had not seen her like this in years.

As the last song was announced Madge suggested we switch it up, and she grabbed Edgar's hand and pulled him onto the dance floor. George and I awkwardly smiled at one another as we followed them for a final dance. I could hear Madge's laughter over the music, and although I couldn't see her or Edgar through the crowded dance floor, I could picture what a good-looking couple they must have made.

Once the dance ended, we went outside to find Madge's father standing beside his car. She thanked George for the evening and said goodbye to Edgar with a little shove to his shoulder.

"You'd better take care of Helen," she said. I walked her over to the car and said hello to Mr. Somers. He gave me a quick nod and opened the door for Madge. The car disappeared into the night as Mr. Somers sped out of the parking lot. It seemed like she was gone as quickly as she had appeared.

Edgar walked me home. We held hands and talked about the different couples we had noticed at the dance. Boys he knew from town and girls I'd recognized from the mill. He wondered if Madge would want to come out on a double date again.

"I don't think so," I said before even thinking about it.

"She really seemed to have a good time," he said. "Maybe we can find someone better than George."

"Maybe." I shrugged my shoulders. I didn't know if I wanted to share all my dates with Madge.

Wedding Bells & Wooden Spoons

Fall 1935

A teapot, a white bowl, and four embroidered pillowcases lay around my feet as a group of girls I hardly knew giggled and drank tea. I was getting married in one week, and Nancy Smith was throwing me a wedding shower at her mother's house. I worked with her at the mill and her fiancé worked with Edgar. I watched Nancy smiling and laughing across the room and couldn't help but notice she was much more excited about the upcoming nuptials than I was.

Time moves like a speeding freight train when you are young. You are eager to get where you're going but can't enjoy the view because it moves so unbelievably fast. One minute you think you are falling in love and the next you are getting married. After I started seeing Edgar, the years rolled by as I took for granted the fortune that is youth. Now here I was, barely twenty years old, about to be married. I couldn't believe it. I wanted to be with Edgar and get away from my mother, but what did I know about being married or being a wife? I did know that this was the expected next step, and Edgar seemed crazy about me. I never dreamed a man would love me like that, think I was beautiful and want to be with me forever. It seemed the only thing to do was get married.

"You've landed yourself a real charmer, Helen." Sybil Reid turned to the other girls. "And he's so handsome! Don't you think so, Madge?" The girls turned to look at Madge, who sat picking tobacco off the tip of her tongue.

"Helen's the luckiest girl I know." Madge turned to flick her ashes in an ashtray I had just opened. She looked as miserable and out of place as I felt. She kept her eyes down. We had not even had a chance to speak to each other since she'd arrived.

My mother sat opposite me on the sofa. She quietly inspected every gift as it was opened and passed it along. She was happy at the thought of having Edgar as a son-in-law. I started to feel the urge to run. My heart was racing, and it felt like there was no air left in the room. I focused on the wooden spoon in my hand and tried to calm my breathing. All I could hear was the buzz of the other girls and the pounding of my heart in my chest. *What am I doing?* was all I could think. *How can I get married? I can't even bake a cake.* I felt a hand on my knee. Aunt Gertie kneeled beside me with a knowing grin on her face.

"It'll be all right, lovey," she said. She told the girls I needed some air, and took me outside. She lit a cigarette and tried to hand it to me. I shook my head. She knew I wouldn't want my mother seeing me smoke. "If you're old enough to get married, Helen, you're old enough to smoke." I smiled and took a long drag to steady my nerves. "Do you love this boy, Helen?"

"I think so. I feel like a different person around him. It's hard to describe. When I'm with him, it's like I matter." I took another drag of the cigarette, feeling just a bit older as I passed it back to her. "He makes me feel wanted. I sometimes get goosebumps just thinking about him." My hand instinctively touched my cheek, where I knew my face was turning a shade of red.

A smile spread across Aunt Gertie's face as she took another long haul off the cigarette. "I know that feeling," she said, knocking the ashes to the ground and handing the last of it back to me. "I had it with a few fellas back in my day. But the thrill of a kiss and the love of a man are two different things, Helen, and it's hard to tell the difference sometimes. You just want to make sure he's a good man. A kind and loving man. After the kissing is done, and the times get tough, he's still got to make you glow inside, make you feel special, and safe. Does that make sense?"

"Sure, it does." I didn't want her to worry about me. "He says we'll be happy."

She looked skeptical as usual. "You know," she said, "my mother once gave me a piece of advice, and when I look back now I realize she wished someone had given it to her." She took my hand in hers. "She told me you should choose a man who offers *possibilities*. Possibilities for a better life, an easier life, and maybe even happiness. You want a man who offers things other than making your heart race and your legs weak. She told me few women choose wisely."

I tossed the cigarette to the ground and crushed it with the toe of my shoe. "Don't worry about me, Aunt Gertie. He says he's going to treat me like a queen." I gave her a kiss on the cheek and left her in the backyard, the cigarette smoke fading slowly around her as I went back inside to open more presents.

One week later Edgar and I were married in the county courthouse. We only invited a few family members. His little brother, Roland, and Sally, the oldest of his three sisters, stood with us. My mother and Eunie came along as well. Edgar's mother came to the service wearing a grey suit and a thin smile. Edgar's father was not there, and nobody offered an explanation for his absence. I did not invite Aunt Gertie. I told myself it was because we were keeping the ceremony small, but deep down I knew it was because I was ignoring her advice, and I worried she didn't approve of Edgar.

It was a quick and quiet affair followed by cake at my mother's. Edgar's mother borrowed a camera from her cousin and took our picture in front of the rock wall. The cold November wind cut through the air and sent chills straight through me as I held Edgar's arm and smiled into the camera. I never did see the photograph, but as we posed together, side by side, I was reminded of the wedding photo I had once seen of my parents, standing outside Uncle Pat's shop in Boston. My mother certainly didn't look celebratory on that day, but she was most definitely the happiest person at my wedding. Edgar had won her over ages ago and she adored him.

We had a room of our own on Water Street and that is where we spent our first night as a married couple. The melting kisses by the rock wall were no preparation for my wedding night. I thought I would be nervous, but I wasn't. Once the lights went out, we were like two different people. Like animals. I couldn't get enough of him, and he couldn't get enough of me. The entire thing shocked me, and I wondered if this is what it was like for other people. Maybe there was something wrong with me, morally. I heard so many women call it their *duty* that I imagined it must be something most of them disliked.

"Does everyone enjoy this so much?" I asked Edgar as I lay in his arms afterward. The room was quiet and dark, the only light coming from the moon outside the window. He laughed. His answer was another kiss, soft and hard at the same time.

We spent the first three days in bed, ignoring the knocks on our door and only getting up to cook eggs and run a bath. That was our honeymoon. I was too innocent to know it couldn't last forever.

Crystal Decanters

Winter 1936

Madge was waiting at the main gate as I left work. I ran to hug her, but before I could get my arms around her, she held out a small package.

"Your wedding present," she said with a smile. Despite the cold day, she stood in a pair of shoes, no hat, no gloves, and her coat hanging open to the wind.

"You didn't have to do that, Madge." I took the package and tucked it under my arm. "Come with me to our new place and I'll open it up. We won't wait for Edgar; he's working late tonight. I'll make us some tea—you must be freezing."

With the wedding, work, and the shock of being a wife, learning to cook and clean for Edgar, I had not seen Madge since my wedding shower over three months earlier.

When I opened the door to our tiny room, the twisted sheets on the unmade bed seemed to scream at us.

"I'm so sorry, Madge, what a mess." I rushed to pull the blankets back over the mattress. "We didn't get a chance to clean things up this morning before we left for work."

"It's okay," she laughed. "You're married, Helen. No need to blush."

I managed a little laugh and made us each a cup of tea.

"Go ahead and open your present." Madge sat smoking her second cigarette. I slowly opened it, suddenly nervous to have her watching me so closely. Nestled in the tissue paper was a heavy crystal decanter, the kind her father had in their house.

"Oh, Madge, you shouldn't have. This is so fancy."

"I just knew Edgar would love it," she said. "Don't you think?"

"Yes, it's lovely. Thank you." I set it down carefully. "Now, tell me what's new with you."

Madge traced the flowers on my tablecloth with her fingers as her cigarette ash grew and grew. It was dangerously close to falling when she finally spoke. "I have news, Helen." Her eyes remained on the tablecloth. I could hardly hear her.

"What is it, Madge?" I pushed the ashtray closer to her as I watched the ash droop.

"I'm to be married too," she said. She still had not looked up. I was in such shock I reached over and took her hand, knocking the ash onto the tablecloth. It was cold and dry, like the hand of an old woman.

"Who are you marrying? I didn't even know you were seeing anyone!"

"I think you know him." Her eyes slowly raised to meet mine. "It's Gerald Johnson. He works at the bank with my father. We met there one day and hit it right off. My mother thinks he's just the best, and Daddy is really coming around to it now. It's all been rather quick." She was talking very fast, wiping the ash off the table, trying to get it in the ashtray.

"Yes, Madge. I know Gerald very well. He's a wonderful man, and he'll make a wonderful husband." I felt a pain in the pit of my stomach that I knew I did not deserve to feel.

"Well, we're getting married soon, you know. It has to be right away, Helen. Do you know what I mean?" She took her hand from mine and put it on her stomach.

"Oh, Madge." I could see a determination on her face, but also a distinct shame. "Do you want to marry Gerald?"

"Very much," she said.

"Do you love him?" I asked.

"Daddy says it has to be done next week, will you stand with me, Helen?"

I gave her my bravest smile. "Of course I will."

Madge left without touching her cup of tea. I sat at the table and tried to make sense of what she had told me. I wanted to be happy for them, but something was holding me back. I couldn't quite call it regret or jealousy, but something about it didn't sit right.

I told Edgar that night about Madge and Gerald Johnson. Edgar knew Gerald had called on me for almost a year and I could tell he didn't think much of him.

"I just can't believe it," I said. "He was always such a gentleman. He never even tried to kiss me. And now they're having a baby."

"Don't be so naïve, Helen." Edgar poured a bottle of cheap whiskey into his new decanter. "Who's to say she didn't kiss him first?"

Madge's father gave her away in front of the fireplace in their living room. Mrs. Somers, Gerald's mother, and I stood by as the minister joined them in holy matrimony. Edgar worked an extra shift that day, so was not able to stand as a witness. It was quick and simple, much like my own wedding. And once again, the mother of the bride appeared to be the happiest person in the room.

Madge and Gerald lived above A. E. Hunt's shop, just a few minutes' walk from us. I had only seen Madge once in the first few weeks following her wedding. She was suffering from morning sickness and seemed perfectly miserable. One Sunday afternoon as we sat in her kitchen sipping tea, I watched her pale, gaunt face and wondered what she must be going through, having a baby growing inside her. I was about to ask her just that when the bells started ringing from the Catholic church on Prince Street. "Isn't that funny," I said. "I don't remember hearing those bells so clearly before."

Madge smiled for the first time since I'd arrived. "They're calling all the sinners," she said, laughing. "They have to be loud, because most of us are living up in the east end."

I smiled back at her and poured us more tea. "When I lived

in Boston, I was friends with a Catholic family who spent a lot of time in church." I had written Madge about Mary Margaret and the Sullivans. But she had never asked me about them, or showed much interested in my time in Boston.

Madge stroked her teacup. "I once knew a Catholic girl and she told me that every Friday she confessed all her sins, and the priest forgave her." She snapped her fingers in the air. "Just like that, instant forgiveness." As I looked in her eyes, I could see she was falling into a sad, dark place. "And the best part was, the priest can never tell anyone. He has to keep the sins a secret. Do you really think they keep the secrets, Helen? Do you really think they don't tell anyone?"

"I don't know, Madge." I shrugged my shoulders and took another sip of tea. "They must, or nobody would tell them." Madge gave a nod of agreement. "It's funny," I offered, desperate now to change her mood, "but that reminds me of one of Aunt Gertie's stories. She knew a lady who found a way to confess. She made a habit of visiting people on their deathbed and she would tell them her darkest secrets. She always waited till she was sure they were on their way out." I shook my head and smiled, remembering how Aunt Gertie had hooted when she told this story. "Everyone thought she was the kindest and most giving person in the community because she sat with all of those people, right up until the very end."

Madge managed a weak laugh and took a drag of her cigarette. "I guess everyone finds their own way, in the end," she said.

When Edgar got home from work that day, I told him I wanted the four of us to do something together, to get Madge out of the house. He suggested we go sledding up on Wood Street.

"I don't know if that would be the best idea for Madge in her condition," I said.

"Madge is the toughest broad I've ever met. She'll be fine," he said. "The fresh air will do her good, and maybe we can loosen up *the banker* while we're at it."

We camped out on a blanket at the top of the hill, kids running all around us as they pulled their sleds back up the hill and launched them once again from the top. I brought hot cocoa in a thermos. Gerald and I sipped ours as we watched Madge and Edgar climb onto the large sled Edgar had borrowed. Madge was tucked in front, and Edgar's legs curled around her as he adjusted the rails and pushed them off for their third trip down the hill.

"I really didn't want her to go down the hill, you know, because of the baby," Gerald said, shaking his head. "I worry about her, Helen. But I'm learning she has a mind of her own, and if she wants something, she's going to get her way."

I laughed to lighten the mood. He did not seem like the happy boy I had once known. "Yes, that sounds like Madge."

He continued to watch them, a frown on his face.

"I was happy to meet your mother, Gerald. She must be so pleased for you and Madge."

"To be honest, Helen, she and Madge really haven't hit it off. I think they are just very different people." He turned then and finally gave me a smile. "She thinks the world of you, though. She always has."

"But I only met her once, just briefly at the wedding," I looked at him with surprise and he continued to smile.

"Yes, but she heard about you for years, Helen. She knows what a wonderful person you are."

Before I could reply, Edgar and Madge dropped down on the blanket, their cheeks glowing red from the climb up the hill.

"Who's coming next?" Edgar pulled my arm and I agreed to go for one run down the hill. He squeezed me tightly between his legs as he wove his way between the other sleds. It was fun to be acting like a kid again, if only briefly. When we returned, Madge and Gerald sat in silence, both staring off in different directions.

"You two can take a turn," I said, pulling the sled up beside Gerald.

"No, he doesn't want to sled." Madge jumped up and took the rope. She smiled at Edgar. "You take me down again, Eddie, I like how fast you go." And off they went again, leaving the two of us behind.

Gerald turned to me. "Did you ever think this is the life you would be living, Helen?" I could hear the frustration in his voice. He stared at me, looking so forlorn. I had no reply. I found it so hard to see him like this. "My mother always told me how proud my father would have been of me. How he always wanted me to work at the bank with his brother and make something of myself. It seems they had it all planned out for me, before I could even speak or walk. When you are shaped and pushed into a life, a life you never asked for, it's hard to claw your way back out and into the life you really want." Snow had started to fall, and a few snowflakes had caught on his eyelashes. He didn't brush them away, he just looked at me with that questioning look on his face.

"Getting married is a big adjustment, Gerald." I reached over and put my hand on his, our wet mittens sticking together. "I think things will improve for you and Madge. Once the baby comes you two will be so happy, I just know it."

"That's what my mother says." He turned away from me and we sat in silence as we waited for Madge and Edgar to come back up the hill.

Dark Skies

Summer 1937

There was a storm the day Madge had her baby. The stench of the rotting river bottom filled the air as water spilled over the dikes and flooded much of the town. Hundreds of people fled to the mill, and production was stopped as sandbags were stacked against the building in an effort to protect the town's most prized possession. Young Percy Hall from the dye room was swept away by the current when he ignored warnings and went too close to the washed-out bridge. His body was never found. I can still hear his mother's cries when they came to the lunchroom and told her. Long, wailing sounds that reminded me of the nighttime cries that sometimes came from creatures in the logging woods.

Madge waited too long to tell Gerald she was in labour. Maybe she just didn't realize it was time, but in the end, it was too late.

I had just come home from the mill when Edgar came to get me. He was frantic. "Madge needs you, there's no doctor, she needs a woman." He was shaking my shoulders and stammering his words. He looked terrified. "She could die, Helen, she could die!"

I grabbed my coat and we made our way down the street, wading through the flood waters. The rain soaked me through in seconds and the wind made it difficult to walk straight. It was not quite dusk, but the sky was black; an eerie blue light shimmered from behind the storm clouds. I had never seen anything so ominous.

We could hear Madge's screams from the front door, and I realized how useless I would be as soon as I entered her room. Blood was pooling on the bed between Madge's legs. Gerald stood beside her, his face as white as the sheets had once been.

"Get it out of me," she begged, her nails almost ripping through the sheets as she gripped them with all her strength. Her wet curls clung to her forehead and her pale pink nightgown was soaked through with sweat. It clung to her breasts, making her appear naked. I knew we couldn't get her to the hospital in this state. I stood silently as she writhed in the bed, grunting and screaming. Gerald looked at me with frantic eyes, begging me silently to do something. What could I do? I was terrified.

I watched as she gave a final, primal scream and the baby emerged onto the blood-soaked sheets. Nothing seemed right. It lay between her legs, a chalky blue colour, covered in mucus and blood. No sounds, no movement.

"It doesn't look right," Gerald's voice rose in a panic.

"It's dead," Madge said just as the doctor walked in. Her voice was calm and cold. "Get it out of here."

The doctor quickly took out his instruments and cut the cord in silence. He covered Madge with a sheet, wrapped the baby in a towel, and handed it to Gerald. The room was so silent now. Gerald followed the doctor into the kitchen. Madge turned to me. I didn't think she'd even known I was there. "Get me a cigarette, Helen." Before I could speak or move, I heard the strike of a match. Mrs. Somers emerged from a darkened corner of the room. I was shocked to hear her voice. Had she been here the entire time?

"You did fine, baby." She handed Madge a cigarette and stroked her hair. "It's all going to be okay now."

I was the only person crying. Silent tears fell from my face as I left the room. For the first time in years, I thought of little baby Shannon in Boston. How perfect she was. How loved she was. Edgar was sitting in the kitchen facing the wall, his back to the doctor and Gerald. When he turned, his face was grey and he, too, had tears in his eyes. I was not able to look at Gerald. I took Edgar's arm and led him down the stairs. The rain had stopped, and we walked home in silence. We had no words for each other, no comfort or understanding. I looked to the sky and could see the remnants of the strange blue light. I wished it was still raining, so it would wash the night off us, but there was no such luck.

Aqua Velva

Winter 1938

The happy years. That's how I like to remember the first few years after the wedding. Our time spent in that little room is so clear in my memory. The sizzle of eggs on the frying pan. The cold floor on my bare feet. The winter nights snuggling under the covers as the windows encased themselves in intricate patterns of frost. Spring mornings, waking up to the sound of birds outside the window. Edgar always the first to wake, his eyes looking at me as soon as I opened mine. And the hot summer nights, just praying for a breeze to come in the window as we sat down to a meal together. There were good times, I can't deny it.

On Friday nights, before we went dancing, the room filled with the sound of Edgar's dress shoes on the wooden floor. I can still feel the pressure of his arm on my waist as he moved me around the kitchen table. "Practice makes perfect," he said. We had no music, but I felt the vibrations of his humming as I buried my face deep in his neck, breathing in his Aqua Velva aftershave. I was so completely lost in him.

Even the mundane routine of the week became exciting because I had him to go home to every day. I continued to work at the mill and Edgar kept his job driving the delivery truck. We saw my mother and Eunie twice a month for Sunday dinner, and that was more than enough for me. We learned how to look after each other, how to cook, buy our groceries, tend to each other when one of us had the flu or a cold. We were kids growing into adults. We were happy.

The same could not be said of Madge and Gerald. They were like two strangers tied together and set adrift. Madge didn't know what to do with herself and she was not taking to the life of a wife. Cooking and cleaning were of no interest to her. Gerald worked as much as possible and when he was home, he tried his best to look after her. I cared for them both and hated to see them so miserable.

After they lost the baby, they became a constant presence in our lives. I'm not exactly sure how it started, but if Edgar and I were going out to dinner or dancing, they were there. If we went to the pictures, they came with us. If we stayed in to play cards, they came over. We were a strange group, Madge and Edgar talking constantly, both of them drinking a bit more than they should, and Gerald and I watching quietly, letting them tell their stories and have their little jokes.

Madge was the only person who could tease my husband. He couldn't take any kind of criticism from anyone else, but if it came from Madge, he was willing to laugh it off. I once joked he couldn't keep the score straight when the two of us were playing gin rummy. In one motion, his arm wiped the table clear. Our cards and drinks went flying and an ashtray smashed into pieces as it hit the floor. He didn't speak for the rest of the night. I learned my lesson. I never joked about such things again.

The four of us were playing cards at our place on a stormy Saturday night in January. The wind howled outside, and Gerald worried about walking home in the snow.

"It's two blocks, for Christ's sake." Madge lit another cigarette and didn't even look at him when she spoke. She poured another drink and dealt the cards.

Gerald and I were winning. That was no big surprise, as we normally won when we were partners. Edgar tended to have a few extra drinks on nights like this. Never too much. Never enough to remind me of my father. But that night, he'd had a little more than usual.

"Are you drinking away your troubles, Eddie?" Madge winked at Edgar as she gave him his last card. "This must be the Campbell luck coming out." She grinned as she eyed Edgar.

I held my breath. *Oh God,* I thought, *this is it, she's gone too far this time.* That was something Edgar's mother always said about their family—that the Campbell luck is what got her seven kids and a useless, drunk husband. He told me how much he hated when she said it. How it was something his brothers and sisters would say whenever anything went wrong, like they were all cursed. I didn't know if Madge knew this or if she was just talking, being silly and trying to tease him.

Edgar and I once dropped by his mother's on her birthday to take her some flowers. It was the first and last time I was in that house. A few of his siblings were there and his older brother Lincoln had just finished telling everyone about how he'd lost his job. He said it was the *Campbell luck.* Edgar leapt out of his chair and across the room before anyone could move.

"I don't ever want to hear those fucking words come out of your mouth again." He pinned his brother against the wall. "You lost your job cause you're a lousy fucking drunk, Linny."

Everyone remained seated, eating their cake and watching with mild interest. Deke, Edgar's father, looked amused by the shock on my face. He leaned forward in his chair and looked at me with red-rimmed eyes and sunken cheeks.

"They say I'm the one with the temper around here, but you just watch out, little lady." He paused and pointed a shaking hand at me. His drink sloshed over the rim of the glass, staining his pants, and the cigarette ash dangling between his fingers fell to the floor. "This one here," he shifted his gaze to Edgar, "our little Eddie, he's got the biggest Irish temper of us all." He took a quick drag of his cigarette. "Mark my words, he's no saint." Edgar released Lincoln and brushed past his father, almost knocking him out of his chair. He grabbed me by the arm and led me out the door.

That was the scene that played in my mind as I watched Edgar arrange the cards in his hand. He stared at Madge in silence; his face showed no emotion. Gerald and I sat by like ghosts, as if they were the only two in the room. I hadn't even looked at my cards. Before any bets were made, Edgar slapped his hand down on the table, "A full house, Maddie." He grinned at her and his eyes lit up like stars. "Guess you're my luck tonight!" They both broke out in laughter and clinked their glasses before taking another drink.

I let out my breath and realized I had been holding it. I looked across at Gerald. He sat in a trance, staring at me with complete surrender. He was like a trapped animal, and the only one who could release him didn't even realize, or care, that he was hurting. He reminded me of the fox my father and I used to find on his traplines in the woods, scared and alone, waiting for some kind of relief. They would sometimes gnaw off their own leg to escape.

Glazed Ham
& Pineapple

Fall 1938

The rain slowly moved down the windowpane and gathered on the chipped paint of the outside ledge. The wood looked rotten to me, old and dirty. But the glass felt cool against my forehead. I had woken up hot and restless. Edgar was still asleep. His soft snoring could barely be heard over the rain on the roof. My eyes instinctively went to the pot next to the door where we had a leak. No drips yet.

It was sunny on this day three years earlier, the day we were married. I sunk into the chair beside the window and wondered if I would ever get used to the swift passage of time. It was hard to believe how many years had passed without my father, so quickly and so easily. Yet it was strangely comforting to know how adaptive we could be to the new lives we fell into, both the good and the bad. Aunt Gertie had once told me, "Time often bewitches us, and we move forward unaware of the changing seasons." I was beginning to understand what she meant.

My mother had insisted on having us for dinner to celebrate our anniversary. The years had not dulled her shine for Edgar. She still transformed herself into a giggling little girl every time we visited. Eunie and I traded many raised eyebrows and questioning glances in our mutual astonishment at her behaviour around him. And this day, of course, was no exception. She made his favourite meal—or what she believed to be his favourite—glazed ham covered in pineapple slices and red cherries. It was unlike anything we'd eaten in our childhood, but she had tried it once on a Sunday visit and he had made a big fuss and poured on the compliments, so now it was here to stay. My mother knew I hated pineapple, and it was all I could do to get the meal down.

Aunt Gertie and Uncle Johnny were there when we arrived. I was surprised to see them. Gertie had not always been Edgar's biggest fan, but she tried for my sake. "Don't look so surprised, dear." She took me in her arms. "This is a day to celebrate, and I'll take any excuse to see you." She greeted Edgar warmly and we all sat down to eat.

Uncle Johnny was more talkative than usual. He asked Edgar about work and how long he had been driving for the Harvey Brothers.

"Almost six years," Edgar said, not lifting his head from his plate.

"There are some openings down at the post office, if you were ever interested in a change." Johnny glanced at Aunt Gertie as he spoke.

"Those must be good-paying jobs," my mother piped in. Johnny opened his mouth to answer but Edgar cut him off.

"I like the freedom of driving the truck. They let me be and I do my job, it works out just fine." He kept his head down and continued to eat his dinner, but there was an edge to his voice, and the lightness of the celebrations took a turn as a familiar dark cloud rolled in over my mother's house. The only difference this time was that she wasn't the one who'd conjured it.

My mother jumped up to serve Edgar another slice of ham and fished out a bright red cherry to put on his plate. "I think your job sounds just perfect for you, Edgar, and if you have been there all this time, well, they must really appreciate you." She smiled at him and he smiled back.

"Thank you." He took his plate back from her.

My mother shot Johnny and Gertie a look that would shut the eye of a needle and shifted the conversation to Eunie and her new job at the mill office. After dinner, Aunt Gertie steered me out back for a quick cigarette. "Johnny is only trying to help Edgar," she said.

"Why would he think Edgar needs any help?"

"He hears things, dear. I think he thought maybe things were not going so well for Edgar at work."

I shook my head. "He must have heard wrong, Aunt Gertie. Edgar has never said a thing about his job."

"You're right." She smiled as she shrugged her shoulders and took another deep drag on her cigarette. "I must have got it wrong. It's hard to believe three years have gone by. I hear the two of you spend a lot of time with Madge and her husband?" She passed me her cigarette.

I took a quick puff. Edgar didn't like the look of me smoking, so I tried not to do it very often. "We go to a lot of dances together, play cards, you know, that kind of thing," I said. "They live right down the street from us."

"I heard she has become a bit of a drinker." Aunt Gertie went to hand me the cigarette again and I waved her hand away.

"Where do you hear these things? That's just a ridiculous thing to say." I shook my head and looked at her big eyes, round with surprise. "Sure, everyone has a few drinks when we're together on the weekends, but I think that's normal. I think I know what a drinker is." I felt ashamed as soon as I'd said it. I had never said such a thing in my life. Implying that my father was anything but perfect felt like a betrayal to his memory. Truthfully, deep down I did think Madge drank too much, and maybe Edgar too, but I wasn't about to admit it.

"Okay, okay." She squeezed my arm gently. "I must have heard that wrong, too. I just worry about you. I want to make sure you're happy."

"It's my wedding anniversary, why wouldn't I be happy?" I turned to leave, and she grabbed my hand.

"Don't go stomping away. I didn't mean to upset you. You should actually be thanking me. Your mother wanted to use this dinner as an excuse to ask the two of you when you'd be having children. I told her to keep her mouth shut, that it wasn't any of her business."

My cheeks went red, as they normally did when any mention of such things came up. "Why does everyone keep asking me that? Women at work go on about how I haven't gotten pregnant, why I don't have a baby yet." I had not thought much about it. Edgar and I had spoken briefly about children before we were married.

He said he preferred to wait, and I thought that sounded perfectly reasonable, given we were just barely out of childhood ourselves. I didn't even know if he liked babies. I hadn't been around many myself, only little Shannon, so I wasn't sure if I did either. After watching Madge's horrific experience, I hoped I would never find myself in a similar situation. And given Edgar's reaction that night, I could only assume he was terrified at the thought of seeing me go through such an ordeal as well.

Aunt Gertie stubbed out the cigarette with her shoe. "Well, I guess most people just figure it would've happened by now. Most couples can't really avoid it." She paused and looked me in the eyes, "Unless they are trying to avoid it." She raised her eyebrows.

"I don't know what you mean." My voice was getting a little shaky. I was embarrassed and I didn't like looking foolish. "How could you avoid it?"

She smiled and I knew it was a smile for herself, not me. "Oh love, you're still so young." She took me in her arms and hugged me tight. "A man can stop himself from getting you pregnant." She was barely whispering now, so close to my ear it was like a little voice in my head. "He has to stay inside you to make a baby."

And then I knew. Of course I wouldn't get pregnant; Edgar always stopped and pulled away from me. I thought that was normal. Aunt Gertie cupped my face in her hands and kissed me on the forehead. "Don't think you're the first young wife to learn this lesson. There's all the time in the world for babies. You just take care of yourself for now."

My head was spinning and I didn't think I could take one more bit of information. I wanted to go home with Edgar, where it was just the two of us. But you can't unhear things. Aunt Gertie had planted her little seeds, and they stayed inside me, for better or worse. Some grew and some didn't. In the end, she had accomplished what she'd set out to do.

Judy Garland
& The Wedge

Fall 1939

The moment my hand touched the doorknob I knew something wasn't right. I put my ear to the chipped wood and listened. Judy Garland's voice filled the hall with her childlike dreams of "Somewhere Over the Rainbow." I slowly opened the door, just a crack, and peeked inside. There they were, Madge and Edgar, sucking on their cigarettes and staring at a radio on the kitchen table. I pushed the door open and they both turned, giving me the same grin.

"Surprise!" Edgar threw his hands out toward the radio. He knocked it by mistake and the song turned to loud static.

"You've moved the dial, Eddie!" Madge reached over and turned a knob, and the machine went silent. They could see the confusion on my face.

"It's your birthday present, a little early," Edgar said. "It's a radio. The latest style, isn't it small?" He rubbed his hand back and forth on his thigh, something he always did when he was nervous.

Madge jumped up from her seat and steered me into my chair. "Just turn this dial here." She slowly brought the music back into the room. A different song was on now, a country song. It sounded like Hank Snow.

"How could we afford such a thing?"

Edgar's smile faded. "I thought you'd like it." Now the mood in the room had changed, and they both looked at me as if only I could save the day.

"I do like it." I smiled at Edgar. "And thank you, it's a wonderful present." I ran my hand along the woodgrain top and smiled at them both.

Madge put out her cigarette. "I'll get going now." She picked up the two glasses on the table and went to rinse them in the sink. I noticed the bottle of whiskey on the counter. "Won't playing cards be so much more fun, Helen, now that we'll have music?" I nodded in agreement as she backed out the door.

Edgar was still in his chair. He continued to smoke his cigarette and rub his leg. "Why are you home so early, Edgar?" I turned the radio off. "It's Thursday. You normally work late on Thursdays."

He was still looking at the radio, avoiding my gaze. "They let me go, those miserable bastards." His voice was low and angry.

"What do you mean? They fired you, just like that, for no reason?"

"Who knows their reasons, they're so full of shit." He slammed his fist down on the table and the radio jumped. I put my hand on it, so it wouldn't fall to the floor. "Thankfully, I had this before today." He pointed to the radio. "Madge was keeping it hidden for me, so I could surprise you. I saved up for it for your birthday. We thought today might be a good day to give it to you."

"Madge already knew you were fired?" I got up and paced the room. *Why did she know this before me? Why was I kept in the dark like a child while he confided in her?* I stopped and stood before him with my hands on my hips. "When did you say this happened?"

"Just a couple of days ago, honey." He reached for my hand and pulled me to sit on his knee. "I wanted to try and find something else before I told you. But the problem is, nobody's hiring. They're all worried about the war and waiting to see what happens."

This was the first real problem we'd had to face, and I didn't know what to do or say. I put my arms around my husband's neck and let him hold me. "It'll be okay," he said. "I'll look after us, just don't you worry." He kissed my neck and held me tighter. "You've nothing to worry about. Nothing at all."

The next day when I left for work, he was still in bed. When I came home, the whiskey bottle was empty and Edgar wasn't there.

Aunt Gertie was waiting outside our place when I came home from work the next week. She emptied her basket on the table. Bread, eggs, pie, and her specialty, meatloaf.

"What's all this for?" I held the loaf of bread in front of her, as if I didn't already know the answer.

"I ran into Edgar yesterday," she said. "He and Madge were having lunch down at the diner." She smoothed the tablecloth with her hands. "What is going on, Helen? The two of them, acting like they've not a care in the world, while you're working your hands to the bone down at that mill." Her cheeks were scarlet red. I'd never seen her quite so worked up.

"He's looking for a job, Aunt Gertie, he's been looking every day."

She unbuttoned her coat and settled into her chair while I made tea. "Helen, this is hard for me to say, but the word around town is that he's a drinker, and nobody will hire him if that's the case. You know this town: everybody knows everybody's business, and everybody knows he was fired for drinking on the job."

I put the teapot down and sat opposite her at the table.

"Oh, honey." She took my hand in hers. "You must have known."

"I didn't, I really didn't." My eyes were wide and innocent, yet Aunt Gertie gave me a look like she didn't believe me. "I mean, I know he has a drink now and then, and in the last few days, he's been having a few because he's so upset about not having a job, but I never heard about being fired for drinking." I pulled my hand away and sat up straight in my chair. "How do you know this is true anyway?" My voice was starting to quiver. "Half the gossip you hear isn't even right. Madge says the new manager at the truck company is a terrible man. He hated Edgar from the start."

"And again, with Madge. Why is she always here, always with him?" She was talking very quietly now, leaning in. "You can't let anything, or anyone, be a wedge between you and your husband."

The word *wedge* sent my mind wandering and I could hear my

father's voice coming back to me, something he'd told me when I was a little girl. I was always asking to work in the woods with him. Mother said I was too small, too weak. Father said it was the danger of the woods and the swinging axes that kept him from taking me there, not my strength. He said I could cut any tree I wanted, as long as I used a wedge.

"The wedge is a tricky thing," he said. "It evens the play in the woods. The smallest man can do the work of the largest as long as he uses a wedge properly. It may take longer, but he'll still get the job done. Even a small girl like yourself can have the strength to bring down something strong with a wedge. It's a cunning conniver, that one. Most people don't recognize the power of the wedge and how it can break the strongest bonds with constant pressure. One tiny tap repeated again and again can do great damage over time. It's not as noticeable this way, but with time and patience, a wedge can help you cut through anything."

I had both hands around my teacup but I hadn't taken one sip. "Who's the wedge?" Tears started to slide down my cheeks. "You think Madge is the wedge?"

"You need to get control of this situation, Helen. That boy needs to be shaken straight."

Edgar came home again that night with liquor on his breath and no job. I didn't say anything. My head was full of questions about Madge and Edgar and his job. I was feeling lost and confused. Why were Edgar and I not talking about things the way we use to? There was a distance growing between us and it scared me.

The next day it was all irrelevant. We sat at the table as the radio announcer reported Canada was at war. I saw a new kind of fear in Edgar's face then. He turned off the radio and put his head in his hands. "I'm fucked now," he said. All I could think of was my father. I couldn't understand why I could not get his face out of my head. The way he'd look at me and embrace me with his smiling eyes. Edgar and I sat at our little table, together yet apart, as our ghosts and fears filled the room and drowned out the problems of yesterday.

Lilacs

"He'll have to go, won't he?" My mother paced the room and looked from my face to Aunt Gertie's. "Or can he just stay home? But he doesn't have a job. That won't look good." She sank into her chair. "He'll be expected to go." She put her head in her hands and finally stopped talking.

"I don't know," I said. "I don't know anything." I hadn't seen her like this since Russell was young. With my brother married and far away in Boston, Edgar was now the centre of her attention.

"Boys are signing up every day." Aunt Gertie lit a cigarette and leaned back on the sofa. The curls of smoke gathered above her head as she took long, thoughtful drags. "They're young and naïve; it breaks my heart to think what this war will do to them."

"Madge told me Gerald signed up on the first day," I said. They both shook their heads as if he had signed his death warrant. "She seems pleased for him." I took the teapot and refilled the cups.

"That girl has always lived in another world." Aunt Gertie could not hold back her disdain for Madge.

"If that poor boy goes overseas, she may never see him again," my mother said.

"Maybe that's what she wants." Aunt Gertie looked at me.

"Don't say such things," I said. I didn't dare tell them how excited Madge had been yesterday. "I just might move to Halifax and live with my cousin if Gerald is shipped overseas," she'd said. She told me how the city would be full of soldiers and activity.

The posters were everywhere now, urging men to sign up for the war. It was the only thing people talked about. At first Edgar thought he would have a better chance of getting a job, with so many men signing up, but he still had no luck. I came home from work that Friday earlier than usual because my overtime was cancelled. Edgar was home drinking.

"Nobody's going to hire me," he said. "If you don't sign up, they take you for a coward. They'll never hire you then. One guy told me he was going to hire a woman to drive his truck. A woman!" He threw his empty glass in the sink and it shattered, sending shards in all directions.

I took the broom from the corner. "Mr. Danes down at the mill says most of the boys are signing up because they figure the war will be over by the New Year and they won't even see any real fighting, maybe not even get out of training." I kept my head down as I swept the glass and spoke quietly. I didn't want him to think I was pushing him to sign up, but it did come with a small bit of pay. It was getting difficult to make ends meet with only my wages at the end of each week. Aunt Gertie continued to bring baskets of food, and it filled me with shame when she saw the empty liquor bottles Edgar left by the sink. She never said a word.

"What does he know?" Edgar grabbed his coat off the hook. "I'm going up home." He opened the door to leave and Madge stood on the other side, holding a small jar. I wondered if she had been listening.

"I've come to borrow a bit of sugar. Where're you off to, Eddie?" She smiled at Edgar and his mood softened.

"Just up home, to see my mother."

"Do you think she's upset about your little brother?" Madge had come in now and placed her jar on the table. I could smell her perfume as she walked past me. Lilacs. She was all done up like she might be stepping out to a dance. Red lipstick, and a bright blue dress that clung to her many curves.

Edgar stepped back in the room and grabbed Madge by the arm. "Roland? What happened to him?" His voice was panicked.

"He's fine. He's just fine. Nothing's happened to him. It's just that…" She paused and looked at his hand on her arm. "He's signed up for the army. Gerald just heard today. He said he was a brave little guy."

Edgar let go of Madge's arm and backed away from her. He turned and ran out the door, slamming it behind him. I could see the red mark on her arm from where his hand had been.

"Madge, are you okay?"

She looked confused, so I pointed to her arm. "That's nothing." She waved her hand at me. "I'm fine. I just hope I didn't upset him too much. I know how sensitive he is about the war." I just stared at Madge's arm. "I'd better get going," she said, backing out the door.

I woke up that night shortly after midnight to a loud banging on the door. Someone yelled for me to come get my drunken husband. When I opened the door, Lincoln, Edgar's oldest brother, stood in the hallway. He pushed Edgar through the door and wished me luck in a slur of broken words. This was my second time meeting Lincoln. He was gone before I could say two words. Edgar couldn't walk or speak. There was just enough moonlight to make out the shadows in the room. I steered him toward the bed. He passed out as soon as he hit the mattress. I thought about the many times my father had come home in this state and how my mother would rage and scream. But I could only feel sorry for Edgar. I knew once he got a job, this would end, and things would be back to normal. I took off his jacket and shoes and hoped the landlady downstairs had not been woken by all the noise. I even managed to get his pants off. That's when I found the paper. It was crumpled up and shoved down his back pocket. I smoothed it out and took it over to the window. When I pulled the curtains back, I had enough light to read.

It was all there. Name. Age. Address. Height. Weight. Marital status. Edgar's signature on the bottom. He had joined the army.

I reached out for my chair and sat at the table, the paper in front of me. Madge's empty jar still sat where she had set it hours before. I thought I could still smell a hint of her lilac perfume.

Four-Leaf Clovers

I left the train station after Madge and I said our goodbyes to Edgar and Gerald. They were off to Amherst for army training. It was hard to believe, but we would only see them on occasional weekends, if they were allowed to come home. Gerald and Madge didn't embrace as they parted, just a nod and a *good luck*. I couldn't let go of Edgar. Despite his behaviour over the past several weeks, I was still desperately in love with him, and I didn't want him to leave. He looked so handsome. The brown trousers, crisp shirt, tie, and balmoral cap made him appear more mature. All of a sudden he looked like a soldier, a true hero. I held him tight and he pulled my arms down from his neck and said he had to go. He kissed me quickly and as he disappeared into the crowd of uniforms, he turned and yelled to Madge and me, "You take care of her."

Madge left the station quickly, saying she was going to meet her mother, and I was left to walk home alone. It was one of those perfect autumn days, not a cloud in the sky. The light breeze carried the false promise of warmth as it scattered colourful leaves at my feet. It brought back memories of my younger days in the woods, and despite the tears rolling down my cheeks I found myself smiling.

When I saw Aunt Gertie at the corner of Prince Street, I knew it was no coincidence. She gave me her biggest smile and put her arm around me as we walked. "Change is becoming the new normal," she said. "None of us knows what the future will bring; we just have to walk on and keep our heads high."

"I've never been on my own before." I wiped my eyes with my handkerchief.

"You don't look on your own to me." Her arm tightened around my shoulder as she led me up the stairs to make me some tea.

"And how are you really doing, love?" Aunt Gertie poured my tea as she glanced at my cheek. I was always in awe of her, how she seemed to know everything.

"It's a hard time for him." My hand went to my face, where I knew the bruise was still visible. "He's so nervous about going, about being a soldier. I don't blame him. He's scared of dying."

"All men are scared of dying. It's just a rare few that take that fear and turn it on their wives."

"He's a good man. I really believe that, Aunt Gertie." We were drinking out of the teacups she'd given me as a wedding present. They were my favourites, white porcelain trimmed with tiny green four-leaf clovers.

"I was told my father was a good man." She sat down but did not continue to speak until I was looking her in the eye. "My mother told me that again and again. I think she was really telling it to herself more than to us kids. I tried to believe it. I'd watch the things he did, and the things he said, and the way he justified it all. I would hear my mother's words, and I'd say to myself, *He's a good man*. Deep down, I knew it was a lie, but I tried to make it the truth. We all did.

"You see, Helen, all lies are tied to the truth. If you tie that truth up tight enough, it will start to disappear, like a rock inside a ball of twine. Eventually you forget the rock is there. But if you loosen that twine just a bit, the truth will work its way out. Because the truth is always stronger than the lie. It needs to be heard."

She took out her cigarette case and struck a match to her hand-rolled cigarette. After the first long drag, she gently picked a bit of tobacco off the tip of her tongue and continued to speak. "You see, my father was a cruel man, a heartless man. And the day I let that truth loosen its way out was the day I decided I wouldn't be like my mother. No man would ever hit me." With the cigarette still in her hand, she leaned forward and tapped the table with her finger. "If your father were alive to see the way that man treats you, that man would be in the ground." She twisted her cigarette in the ashtray next to the radio, picked up her coat, and walked to the door.

"Don't leave angry, Aunt Gertie. Sometimes I just don't know what to do. I love Edgar and he loves me. He really does. You'll see, the army will be good for him, for us."

She walked back over to me and gently kissed my bruised cheek. "I only care about what's good for you, love."

When the door closed behind her I stared at the hole in the wall, just to the left of the door. I wondered if she had noticed it. Edgar had put his fist through the plaster two nights before. Madge and Gerald had been over that night. We all knew it would be our last time together before they left, but nobody mentioned it. We wanted to forget about the war for just one night. We listened to the radio and played cards. Madge decided she and Edgar should be partners. "That way he won't cheat." She poured everyone a round of drinks.

It was a fun night until the dancing started. Madge had pulled Edgar up from the table when one of her favourite songs came on. We laughed as they danced around the room, and then Gerald grabbed my hand and pulled me up. Everyone had had a few drinks and the room was full of smoke and music. I was a bit tipsy, as I normally didn't have more than one drink. I slipped as Gerald went to spin me and knocked a chair into the table. Edgar's bottle of whiskey fell to the floor. Everyone froze as the liquor spilled under our feet, chunks of glass littered around the puddle. Gerald rushed over and pulled Madge out of Edgar's arms before she could take another step. She was in her bare feet and he carried her to the other side of the room. Edgar had not seen me knock the table, so he wasn't sure why the bottle fell, or why Gerald had grabbed Madge, but his reaction was instant. He grabbed the table and lifted it a good two feet before turning it on its side.

"Jesus fucking Christ!" he yelled as the new radio slammed to the ground and the rest of our glasses crashed to the floor. He took a step toward Gerald.

"Eddie!" Madge reached out to try and calm him, but Gerald pulled her back.

"We're leaving. Will you be all right, Helen?" Gerald had me by both shoulders and was trying to get me to focus on his face. I couldn't hear what he was saying. "Helen." He shook me and I saw the concern on his face.

I managed a nod and said they should go. "I'll be fine," I said.

"Oh, she'll be just fucking fine," Edgar yelled as they left. "You'll be just fine after you clean up this mess, won't you? That bottle was a gift from my father. My send-off!" His eyes were wild, and I could see now how drunk he really was.

I reached out for his hand. "Edgar, I—" Next thing I knew, I was on my knees. My ears were ringing, and my right cheek was on fire. He had slapped me hard across my face.

I stayed there with my head down. I don't know if I was scared or shocked, but I didn't move. He muttered under his breath and I heard a loud sound that made me think he had broken something else. I stayed where I was, the door slammed, and I could hear him stumbling down the stairs. When I looked up, there was a hole in the plaster the size of a fist.

The next morning, the room looked as it always had. The radio was back on the table, and despite the fall, it still worked. Edgar came home after lunch. He was showered and shaved, and I could smell the lingering hints of corned beef and cabbage from his jacket when he put it on the back of my chair. It was the smell of his mother's house. He had a box of chocolates with him and a long list of apologies. He cried. He told me he was scared to leave me, that he couldn't control himself when he got so upset. He was going to cut back on the booze. He was going to make everything better. I believed him. I forgave him.

I looked down now at my teacup and ran my finger along the little green clovers. I stared at the hole in the wall and remembered his tears.

"He's a good man, Aunt Gertie," I spoke to the empty room. "You'll see."

Wedding Rings

Winter 1940

Four months after training camp started, Madge's father had a stroke. She'd gone home to help look after him, but he passed away the day after she arrived. I went to her as soon as I heard. Walking up the familiar drive my head filled with memories of the days when Madge and I ran down this lane, making daisy chains, chasing butterflies, and racing home for cookies and milk. It seemed like so long ago.

My smile faded when I saw him sitting on the front porch, a hat pulled down over his eyes. He was in his mechanic overalls, legs stretched out in front of him like he owned the place. The smell of diesel and dirt filled my nose before I reached the porch. As my foot hit the first stone step he threw his cigarette butt, just missing my shoulder. I kept my eyes on the big brass door knocker. I had not seen Madge's brother since that day in his truck so long ago. The same day my father died. I felt an unexpected surge of anger as those memories came rushing back. I could feel my face turning red. I thought if he spoke one word to me, I just might spit in his face. I walked up the steps, eyes straight ahead, and walked through the front door. It was the first time I'd never knocked. I felt his gaze on me like a rifle's scope.

Mrs. Parsons appeared in the front hall. "Well, I thought I heard the door. Look at you, Helen, all grown up. A married woman now, and still working at the mill. So much like your mother." She gave a little laugh. "I hear your husband is off with Gerald, training in

Amherst." She paused to look around and see if anyone was listening. "They say Gerald will most likely become an officer."

"I came as soon as I heard about Mr. Somers," I said.

"Oh yes, so fast, but fast is best." She stepped closer. "Mrs. Somers has been in bed since it happened." She lowered her voice even more. "The doctor said she needed sedating."

"Where's Madge?" I started toward the kitchen.

"No, she's up in her room." Mrs. Parsons pointed up the stairs. "She'll be happy to see a friendly face."

Madge sat on the edge of her bed, staring out the window, an old rag doll in her hands. The room was just as I remembered it. Everything looked the same, except Madge. I sat down and put my arms around her.

"I'm so sorry, Madge." I remembered when my father died and nobody wanted to see me cry or grieve. I wanted to help Madge through this.

"It is what it is, Helen." She turned and looked at me. Her eyes were dry. No red rims, no sign of sadness. "I've got to get out of here." She stood and went to pick up her suitcase. "Thanks for coming, though. I don't deserve you, Helen; I don't think I ever have." She started to pack her suitcase, shoving things in with such force I thought she might rip her clothes.

"Do you really want to leave right now, Madge? What about your mother?" I went to the doorway and looked down the hall, as if she might be coming to find us at any moment.

"I'll never sleep in this house again. She has her son back now. I think that's all she ever really wanted."

I stood by the bed, unsure of what to say. Madge and I had only seen each other a few times since Edgar and Gerald left for training. I now felt guilty for not making more of an effort. When she was ready, we walked out the front door without a word to Mrs. Parsons or Mrs. Somers.

He was still on the porch. I knew Madge didn't like her brother, but I was not prepared for the pure hatred I could feel in the air. It was like a living, breathing thing that took up all the space around us and drowned out the rest of the world. The only noise that cut through the silence was the high-pitched whistle that came from his lips. We were halfway down the drive when we heard him.

"Bye-bye, now, little sister."

Madge's step faltered only slightly. She kept walking, head held high, suitcase in hand and a look of determination I had never seen before. Neither of us spoke the entire walk home. When I dropped her at her place, I gave her a hug and told her I would come see her the next day.

"If you want, Helen, but I'll be fine." She looked so much like her mother. The same sad eyes, the same lost soul.

I went every day. If I worked, I went afterwards. If I didn't, I was there all day. The strength Madge had shown at her mother's house withered. She was a lost little girl with no one to help her but me. I fed her. I cleaned for her and I shopped for her. I sat with her when she drank too much, and I sat with her when she cried. She never spoke of her father, or her sadness. She was just trying to get to the other side of it all and I understood that.

After a week, I arrived early on a Saturday morning and told her we were going shopping. "I want to buy something for Edgar," I said. "I want to give him my wedding ring, so he'll always have me with him. If I buy a chain, he can wear it around his neck."

"Oh, Helen." She shook her head and looked at me. "Edgar doesn't know how lucky he is. None of us deserve you. You're just too good for us all."

"Don't be silly." I took a dress out of the closet and threw it at her. "Put this on."

While Madge dressed, I thought about Edgar. He had only made two visits home in the past four months and they had both been terrible. His drinking, his temper, and his violent outbursts were becoming too much for me. I'd had to miss work once because of the bruises on my face. He always apologized, and I always forgave him. "It will be better when we're back together," he said. "When this war is done, and I'm home again, it will be back to the way it was." I tried to believe him. I thought if he were home with me all the time, he wouldn't behave like this. He just needed me with him.

The brass bell mounted at the top of the door rang as we entered the store. I quickly realized if Madge had not been with me, I may not have gone in by myself. It was so intimidating. Dark red carpet covered the floor and gleaming glass cabinets lined both sides of the long, narrow space. A deep mahogany counter ran the length of the back of the shop and silver candlesticks and bowls were displayed on shelves that reached the ceiling. The man behind the counter was dressed in a three-piece navy suit. He was a precise-looking little man: perfectly combed hair, round spectacles, and tiny feminine hands. I asked him to show me a gold chain.

"These are quite expensive, Miss." He looked from my hat to my coat and back to my hat again. A light snow had just started before we reached the shop and a dusting of snowflakes still rested on my hat and shoulders. He glanced at Madge, put on a pair of white gloves, and took out a large velvet box. Little did he know, I was the top seamstress in my division. Each week I had more coupons than any other girl, and I had been secretly saving a portion of my pay for two years. And littler still did he know, even a girl from the backwoods could save and plan and, bit by bit, make things happen. I bought the chain and decided I would never enter that shop again.

Madge looked very pleased for me as we left. She smiled at me for the first time that week.

"Now I'll have a surprise for Edgar when he comes home on his next visit." I tucked the package in my purse.

"I'm taking you to lunch!" Madge locked her arm through mine and we set off for the diner. There was a bit of a bounce back in Madge's step and it was almost like the old days. Almost. I glanced back at the shop one last time when we reached the other side of the street. Our footprints marked a lonely path across the newly fallen snow. It made me sad to know we could never go back to the old days. We could never be the young, carefree girls we once were. We were married women now, with dead fathers, and husbands about to go to war.

White Carnations

Fall 1940

It rained through the night and the autumn leaves lay motionless on the damp, cool ground. The smell of their decay filled the air. The hovering maples that gave shade in the summer were now bare and their stark branches provided no protection over the crowd gathered at the train station.

I knew. As soon as I saw him, I knew something was wrong. I knew things were going to change. People rushed by him on the platform. He stood still. His shoulders slumped forward and his head was slightly down. He looked lost. His bag was on the ground, at his feet. His eyes peered up from under his cap as he scanned the crowd, jerking his head left and right. This was not the confident man I had watched week after week, year after year, wait for me at the rock wall.

I stepped forward and called his name. Edgar looked toward me but remained still. I ran to him and threw my arms around his neck.

"I missed you." I slipped back down to the ground and a familiar smell hit me. Stale whiskey, sweat, and cigarettes. This was a smell from my childhood. A smell I'd wanted to forget. His arms hung at his sides. I held his face in my hands and looked into his glassy eyes. "How are you?"

"Tired and filthy." He looked beyond me at the thinning crowd. "Let's get home." He slung his bag over his shoulder and took my hand. I could see the bandage on his other hand as he held the bag in place.

The walk home was quiet. He didn't speak and I was so nervous I would say the wrong thing, I just kept squeezing his hand and saying how wonderful it was to have him home.

He took a bottle out of his bag as soon as we entered our place, and poured himself a large glass of whiskey. I said nothing. He dug in his pocket and took out some pills. He washed them down with the liquor. He could see me watching him. "They're for the pain." He held up his bandaged hand to show me. "Fucking training exercises."

I nodded and took the frying pan out. "What can I get you? You must be hungry."

By then he was done his second drink and his eyelids were droopy. "I'm hungry all right, but not for eggs." He rose from his chair awkwardly, knocking it over. He stumbled forward, grabbed my wrist, and pulled me to the bed. His grip was tight, and I pulled back.

"I'm having my monthly, Edgar." My voice a whisper. "I'm sorry." I put my hand on his bandage. "We'll just have to wait. Just a day. Today should be the last of it."

He threw me down on the bed and undid his belt. "I'm going to war, Helen, I'm not waiting." He reached up my skirt and pulled down my panties. I was mortified as my blood-stained rags came with them; he threw them off to the side. He lay on top of me. The pressure of his full weight nearly took the air from my lungs, and the stench of his warm, stale breath mixed with the putrid odour of his filthy uniform was suffocating.

"Please," I whispered. "Not like this."

Tears filled my eyes and he looked at me like he didn't know me. Like he couldn't even see me. He rose, picked me up, and quickly turned me over. He kept one hand on the back of my head. My neck was twisted awkwardly to the side. The window was open and I could hear the Sampson boys next door playing in the yard, calling back and forth to each other, chasing a ball. All I could see was the legs of the kitchen table, the overturned chair, and his army bag half open on the floor. I stared at the dirty bag. I didn't move. How could he ruin this for us? I thought, over and over. It would never be the same.

When he was done, he buttoned his pants. His voice was softer when he spoke, yet I heard no regret in it. "I have to visit my mother, she'll be waiting." I remained face-down on the bed. I said nothing. When I heard the door close, I rolled to my side and pulled my knees up to my chest. I could feel something running out of me, down my thighs. I knew it was more than blood. Aunt Gertie's voice rang through my ears: *He has to stay in you.* This was the first time he had. I cried quietly and rocked myself on the bed. *What will happen now?* I thought. *What will become of us now?*

The bedding was stained with blood. I tried to wash it, but my hands would not stop shaking. I found a new bedcover in the closet. I tried to make the room look normal again. Like none of this had happened.

Edgar returned just before supper. He was showered and whistling as he came through the door. I was sitting at the kitchen table, where I had been for hours, staring at my hands. I had never felt so cold.

"Get dressed, little lady. I'm taking you out to dinner."

There was no trace of the man who had been here earlier that day. He had a bouquet of flowers and a big smile. He put the white carnations on the table. I rose and went to change my dress for dinner.

We never spoke of that morning, and I'd never know if he even remembered it. I thought maybe I could forget it, but I was wrong. There was never a time we were in bed again that I did not think of it. He'd destroyed something in me. I didn't know exactly what, but something in me was crushed that day and I was sure it would never come back again.

Long Underwear

Spring 1941

With Edgar away, I had nothing to do except work. I was still sewing at the mill and I took extra shifts whenever possible. My speed and reputation were well known, and I was often asked to help out in other areas when production was falling behind. I was grateful to keep busy. The radio Edgar gave me turned out to be a blessing, as the music and voices helped to fill the unbearable silence of the lonely nights at home.

Since the beginning of the war, new people were being hired constantly and the mill was busier than I had ever seen it. I was asked to work weekends, helping to sew labels on woollen blankets. The word was these were for the war. During lunch break, one of the new girls began telling us stories about her uncle who'd worked in the dyeing room for years. She told some funny ones about boys turning their hands blue and silly things that most of us had heard before. Everyone laughed along with her. She was young and wanted to fit in.

"Apparently one lady had some real sticky fingers," she said. "They thought she was stealing. They suspected her for quite some time, but nobody did anything about it. One day when she was leaving, they pulled her up to the office. One of the secretaries had to be there, 'cause she was a woman and all, and they asked her to lift her dress! Well, wouldn't you know it, she had three pair of men's long underwear on!" She slapped the table for affect and started to laugh. It took her a few minutes to realize nobody else was laughing with her. "Her name was Kendall, or Cameron or something like that." She looked from face to face, trying to pull her audience back in.

A few girls in the room glanced at me when she finished her story, knowing she was speaking about my mother-in-law. I finished my tea and smiled back at the girls. Luckily, before the young one could speak again, the bell rang and we all rose in silence to return to our machines.

What the new girl didn't know was that we all knew stories like this. Stories of people stealing or cheating with their coupon books. I never knew of anyone fired for such behaviour. In fact, more often than not, if someone was found stealing, they were back at work the next day like nothing had ever happened. Sometimes, the families involved would find a box of food on their back step. No questions asked. It was never confirmed that old man Stanfield sent these boxes, but we all knew he did. He looked after his own. He knew people had hard lives and sometimes made bad choices. So, his workers remained loyal. The new girl didn't know this yet; she didn't realize we were like a family: we might fight and disagree, but we always remained loyal.

A few days later I was having dinner at my mother's. Eunie was not home, but Aunt Gertie was there. I asked her what she knew about my mother-in-law. Margorie Campbell and I hardly knew each other, and she'd shown no interest in me. Aunt Gertie told me Deke Campbell was a mean-spirited man and that life was more than hard for his wife. "She was the main breadwinner in that family. She had to feed all those kids, seven of them! And put up with his drinking and abuse. The poor thing had no other choice—where could she go? She had no family of her own. Just that miserable excuse for a man." My mother sat beside us, listening but not offering an opinion.

I told them about the story from work. "I know that story," Aunt Gertie said. My mother nodded that she knew it too. "But," Aunt Gertie continued, "the part most people don't know is that when that stick-thin little woman took off the underwear—just in front of the secretary, mind you, not the men—that poor woman was covered in bruises, all over her legs and stomach. No one said a word about it; she was given the underwear to take home in a bag and told to come back to work the next day." She paused. She could see I had been looking down at my hands, twisting my handkerchief. When I looked up, Aunt Gertie caught my eye and continued. "You see, he never hit her in the face. He didn't want anyone seeing his work. He'd been doing this for years and he knew better than to raise suspicions."

My mother got up from the table and took our plates. "I always liked Marjorie Campbell. She's a good worker, I know that. And look at the wonderful boy she raised in our Edgar." She looked at me with a rare smile and I was again amazed at how much she cared for him.

When my mother left the room, Gertie took my hand in hers. She lowered her voice. "I'm sure Edgar has seen his share of hard times under that roof, just as your father witnessed under our own when he was a boy. But the lesson your father took from it was to be a kind and gentle man. I worry what lessons Edgar has learned from his father."

She had only ever once seen a bruise on me. I had been careful not to let anyone see them again. Over the past year, Edgar's visits had been more and more erratic. I never knew who was going to come through the door. Would he be calm and loving, or drunk and abusive? More often it was the latter, and I found myself dreading his weekend leave.

I pulled my hand away. "Don't worry, Aunt Gertie. I'm no Marjorie Campbell." My voice was unsteady, and I worried I didn't sound very convincing. "Please excuse me, I'm going to go help with the dishes." I followed my mother to the kitchen and tried to leave Aunt Gertie's words behind me. But as she was well aware, once spoken, they were hard to forget.

Pomade & Manila Envelopes

Summer 1941

I was shocked to see Edgar sitting on our front step that day.

"I asked for special permission to visit you." He took my hand and held it. "I needed to see you one last time. We leave for Europe in two days."

I wrapped my arms around him and snuggled into his neck. I breathed in his aftershave and was relived I couldn't smell a trace of whiskey. I made him dinner and we talked more than we had in months. It was the Edgar I had married: no drinking, no temper, just the two of us dancing and making love.

When I opened my eyes in the morning, he was standing at the end of the bed watching me. I could see the gold chain with my wedding ring tucked behind his collar. "I have to go." His voice was just above a whisper. I thought I might cry, so I bit my lower lip and tried my best to stay calm. He placed an envelope on the bed. "I need you to go to the doctor, Helen."

I sat up quickly. "Do you think I might be pregnant?" It was the only reason I could think of for going to the doctor.

He rested his hand on my leg. "No, I don't think you're going to have a baby. I think you may have something some of the guys at the barracks have." His words trailed off and he was now looking at the envelope. "Some of their girls, too." He sat down beside me. "I don't know much; I was just told that you need to go to the doctor. His name is written on this envelope, and you need to give him these papers." I went to take the envelope, but he took my hand. "Don't read them, they're for the doctor." Now I could see. He wasn't upset about leaving me, he was upset about the envelope. His face was full of shame. He let my hand go and started to rub his thighs. "I really don't know much about it, but we were all told to send our wives to the doctor."

I went to pick up the envelope again. "Edgar, I…" He put his hand over mine so I couldn't take it. He leaned over and kissed me. "I have to go." As he walked out the door, he looked back one last time. "It's not what you think." He closed the door and was gone.

Edgar and the rest of the North Novas set sail for Europe and I was left behind to deal with the envelope. I knew I must do as he said and go to the doctor, but I felt the innocence Edgar once said he loved about me being chipped away, one little piece at a time.

Two weeks later, I went to Halifax. Edgar had once brought Madge and I to the city for a day of exploring so I was not nervous about finding my way. The city was large, loud, and bustling, but it was nothing compared to my memories of Boston. I asked a man at the train station for directions, and took a trolley to a large building with the street number that matched the one written on the envelope.

A nurse took my name and led me into an office. "Dr. Lorimer will be here shortly," she said. I handed her my manila envelope. She put it on the desk, closed the door, and left me alone. I had been staring at that envelope since the day I got it. I'd never opened it because I had been told not to. Now, looking at it on the desk, I could still feel the weight of it in my hands. I put my purse on my lap and folded my hands over it, trying to stop them from shaking. My mind was racing—*Why am I here? What has Edgar done?* Why did I feel shame when I didn't know what was going on? Edgar would be the death of me, I just knew it. I felt so low I thought I might melt right out of my chair and seep through the floorboards. I had never been examined by a doctor before.

The door opened quickly. The papers on the desk fluttered and settled back down. The doctor walked past me to his desk and picked up my envelope. He took out the papers and read them with his back to me. His black hair was slicked back with precision and his white starched coat shone under the single bulb overhead. A perfect crease travelled the length of his grey trousers, right down to his cuff, which rested on perfectly polished black shoes.

"Is it Mrs. or Miss?" His back still to me.

"I'm married."

"Please speak up, I'm going to need to hear everything you have to say."

"My name is Mrs. Edgar Campbell."

"Well, Mrs. Edgar Campbell," he turned to face me, his cigarette clung to the side of his mouth while he talked, "someone in your nuptial union has not been faithful, and this act has brought venereal disease into your home. It seems that both you and Mr. Edgar Campbell have syphilis." He waved the letter in front of me, then threw it on his desk. "According to this letter."

"Well, I—" I started, but he cut me off.

"I don't care what kind of story your husband has spun for you, Mrs. Campbell, but there is only one way to catch this, and it's fornication. You will now need to undergo several months of treatment." I stared at his black shoes, wondering if I might see my shocked face reflected back at me. "Do you understand?" I looked up into his tiny dark eyes, which were sunk behind his bulbous nose. His cheeks were scarred with deep pockmarks, and his eyebrows were full of dandruff. I stood and realized we were the same height.

"It could not be clearer," I said.

He closed the door, had me strip naked and lie on a metal table. My skin was covered in goosebumps. I lay my arms across my chest to cover my erect nipples as he poked at my privates with his fingers. "No question," he said. "You have it." He then made notes on his clipboard and read my file again. He told me to sit and he stood behind me, massaging my breasts with his clammy hands. I could feel the buttons from his lab coat pressing into my back and the smell of his pomade cream and cigarette made me noxious. My eyes were shut tight, but the tears managed to escape; when I opened my eyes, I could see them landing on his hands. He continued to make small humming noises.

The nurse knocked on the door loudly. "Doctor?"

He abruptly stopped. "We're almost done," he shouted. I stared ahead. Streams of light filtered through the window blinds and I could see particles of dust suspended in the light. *These are not God's lights*, I thought.

"Get dressed." He said as he walked out of the room, leaving the door slightly open. I jumped up and shut the door. It took me three tries just to get my shaking legs into my stockings. I was putting on my shoes when there was a soft knock.

"Mrs. Campbell, it's the nurse. Are you decent?"

"Come in." I pulled my coat on as she came in. Her eyes told me everything. She knew what kind of man that doctor was.

"From now on, you'll only see me," she said. "I'll give you the medicine every week and we'll flush your eyes as well, to prevent blindness."

"Blindness!" I sank back in the chair.

"Don't worry, Mrs. Campbell, it's just a precaution. The treatment will take six to eight months. Is there anyone you could stay with here in Halifax? I see you live in Truro." I must have nodded because she looked pleased. She handed me a handkerchief. "Someday, when this is all over, it will be like it never happened." I wished I could believe her.

As I walked back into the waiting room, I noticed a small woman about my age, awaiting her turn with the doctor. She looked up and our eyes briefly met. Two strangers exchanging an immeasurable amount of shame in one short glance. I tried to understand how my life had come to this moment. I thought of Edgar's last words to me: "It's not what you think." He gave me more credit than I deserved. I hadn't thought anything. I hadn't known enough to think such things. Now I knew different. If only my mother could see me now, how would she feel about her precious Edgar?

Red-&-White-
Checkered Napkins

I left the mill and found a job at a uniform factory in the city. I didn't like Halifax and as the weeks turned into months, I knew I never would. My mother didn't know the truth of why I'd left. I told her I wanted a change, a new job and a chance to be closer to Madge. All lies. But the lies were easy because I didn't have to look her in the eye. I rarely looked anyone in the eye anymore. I worked and went for treatments.

Aunt Gertie suspected there was more to the story, but she let me be. She came to visit me after I'd been in the city for two months. I surprised us both when I told her, over tea, that I was going to leave Edgar. "When he comes back from the war, I don't want to be his wife anymore."

"Thank the Lord! That man has his own devils to fight, Helen, and you can't help him. From the moment I met him, I knew he was trouble. You couldn't trust his shadow, that one." She paused and finally noticed my tired, sad eyes. "Oh, I'm so sorry, love." She took my heartbroken face in her hands. "You may not believe this now, but life has more than one love for us all. Some day, maybe not any time soon, but some day, you'll look up and be surprised to realize you love somebody else, and even more surprised at how easy it is to be happy." I knew I should believe her, but it was hard. "In the meantime, make sure you keep getting Edgar's army pay. You're still his wife, and he owes you."

I lived in a boarding house with six other women. Some were

single and, from what I could tell, always on the lookout for a man. The landlady called us the "in-betweens": married without children or husbands, just waiting for the men to return and get us pregnant, so we could move on with life. I didn't like her assessment of our situation. Everyone else seemed nice enough, but it was not a time to make friends, it was a time of survival, and without Edgar's pay I would not have survived. The other ladies never spoke about the war wages, but I could only imagine we all received them. I didn't know them well enough to ask.

When she'd left Truro, Madge told me she was going to use Gerald's wages to help pay her way in Halifax. That was so long ago. I had not seen Madge since I'd come to Halifax. After leaving several messages at her cousin's house, I finally had a note back from her.

We met for coffee on a Saturday. I arrived early and the waitress brought my coffee and set two red-and-white-checkered napkins on the table. I took one in my hand and smiled as I remembered my father and the first mountain I ever saw. It rose from the ground and almost touched the clouds. I stood holding my father's hand, my eyes wide and my mouth gaping.

"That looks like a fine place to have a picnic," my father said as he took my hand and pulled me up the mountain. Of course, I quickly realized the mountain was a pile of sawdust. No doubt the largest sawdust pile in history, but a mountain to a girl on her first big trip out of the woods. Father had brought me with him to visit another sawmill. He'd borrowed a truck from a man he worked with and we'd driven for miles and miles through winding roads to reach this place, which was so like our own mill and yet so different. More men, more wood, more activity and, of course, more sawdust.

When we reached the top of the mountain I looked back over the endless view of trees, knowing our home was in there somewhere. My father took my shoulders and gently turned me around. "This is what I wanted you to see, Helen, take a look at that." At first, I was confused; I thought the trees had fallen into the sky. "That's the ocean," he said.

"Is it really?" I asked. He laughed and opened up our lunch. He had packed all my favourite foods: biscuits, cheese, and pickles. We even had a thermos of lemonade.

"I'll drive you to see the ocean after we eat," he said.

I really can't recall what it felt like to first walk in the water, or hear the waves. Those memories did not hold. What stayed with me is my father's smile on top of the sawdust pile as he laid out our picnic and placed a little red-and-white-checkered napkin on my lap.

I watched a man in a black car pull up outside the diner. A woman got out and it took me a few seconds to realize it was her, but I would have known that walk anywhere. She was skinny, and her dress hung off her like a sack. Her makeup was smudged and a cigarette hung from her bright red lips. It was her hair I was staring at when she reached the table. It was jet-black. Her beautiful blond curls were gone. It was the first time I had ever known anyone to dye their hair.

"I know, I know, I can see the shock on your face." She ran her hand down the side of her head. "But it's still me, still the same old Madge. I just needed a change." She sat down opposite me, and I found myself feeling at home for the first time since coming to this city. Black hair or not, Madge was Madge, and just being with her somehow always made me feel better.

She went into vivid detail about the dances she went to, her nights at the Ajax Club and the soldiers she met there. She showed me a little advertisement card for the dress shop where she worked and then mimicked the voices of the rich ladies who came to the shop to gossip about each other and buy expensive dresses. She smoked with one hand and picked at her napkin with the other. She handed me a picture of her cousin and described how hard it was for her to care for her aunt, who was in a wheelchair. She insisted she was happy before I had the chance to ask. I couldn't believe her. Despite her smile and energetic talk, the dark circles under her red-rimmed eyes and the trembling of her hands as she lit her cigarette told me a different story. She looked sad and lost, like the Madge from our youth often did. She didn't mention Gerald once, but she did ask about Edgar.

"I've not had one letter from him." Without meaning to, I began to cry. I'd never confided in Madge before about anything between Edgar and me. I was never one to discuss my private affairs, and neither was Madge. But on that day, it all came spilling out. I told her how unhappy I was here in the city. How poorly Edgar had treated me the year before he left. How I now knew him to be a dishonest person. I didn't tell her about the treatments. I could never tell anyone about that. "I don't think I can ever be with him again, Madge." As soon as the words were out of my mouth, I held my breath. Other than what I had told Aunt Gertie, I had never spoken of leaving Edgar. And I knew Madge and he were friends. She liked him. I worried she would tell me to give him another chance.

She leaned over the booth and reached for my hand. "You have to do what you have to do to make yourself happy, Helen." She sounded wiser than her years. "You, beyond anyone I know, deserve to be happy and away from the people who hurt you." Tears slipped down her cheeks and she wiped them away with the back of her hand in the quick, exasperated motion of a small child. I had never seen her like this. "I've got to get going." She put some bills on the table. "Be happy, Helen. One of us should be."

I watched her leave. I thought she would catch the trolley car that was coming up the street, but she kept walking. I followed her progress and then I saw the black car parked farther up the street. She got in the passenger seat and it drove away. I held my napkin in my lap and traced the red-and-white-checkered pattern with my finger. I looked across the table at the remnants of Madge's napkin, a small pile of pulp, torn to bits, now beyond recognition. The strangest feeling came over me, like a cold breeze up my back. My mother use to call it the *death chill*. I worried I would never see Madge again.

When my treatments were done, I wrote Mr. Stanfield and asked if I could have my job back. I knew my boss, Mr. Quinlan, would understand. He often commented on how sad I looked at work. "You need to get out. You're young, go to the pictures!" He was pleased with my work, but I would be happy to never see a brass button again. I didn't know if Mr. Stanfield would even know who I was. I figured I had nothing to lose, and the worst he could say was no. I was miserable here in this dirty, crowded city and I craved something familiar, something from my old life.

Within three weeks, there was a letter waiting for me with *Stanfield's* embossed on the envelope. I opened the letter slowly and with a sense of dread, sure I would be looking at those brass buttons for the rest of my days. I read it three times. By the time I started on the fourth, my cheeks were aching from the smile on my face. They wondered if I would be interested in taking a job at a smaller mill they owned in Amherst, as a supervisor, to help with the overflow of war orders. I wrote my reply and packed my bags that night.

Peppermints & Poetry

Spring 1943

I spent my first year at Amherst Woolens wading through a fog. I was there in body but unwilling, or unable, to commit any other part of myself. I wanted to be there, to start a new life, to meet new friends and find a bit of happiness, but I just couldn't seem to do it. I worked hard and was well respected, but I couldn't connect with anyone.

In the beginning, other girls tried to befriend me by inviting me out to lunch or the pictures, but after so many no-thank-yous and excuses, they gave up on me. I told myself I couldn't be lonely, because I had chosen to be alone. I didn't want to be around anyone, not family or coworkers. But in truth, I was desperately sad and lonely. I went through the motions and watched myself living the life of an old lady. My mother's life. I wanted to get out of the fog. I wanted to laugh, to smile, to feel the urge to have fun again. It was a surprise that a loudmouth like Janice Walker and a wallflower like Ruth Cameron would be the ones to set me free.

At the mill in Truro, we had talkative ladies and quiet ladies. Amherst was no different. Our lunch breaks were often spent either listening to Janice, or trying to block out her constant commentary. She loved an audience, and she loved the sound of her own voice even more. About a year after I arrived, another outsider came to the mill. Her name was Ruth Cameron. Most of the workers were born and raised in the Amherst area. When people came from away there was always a certain amount of speculation and suspicion.

Because I came as a supervisor, I wasn't exposed to this scrutiny in the same way a regular floor worker like Ruth was. For her entire first week, Ruth sat in the corner of the lunchroom and read a book during her breaks. This was too much for Janice. After five days of watching her sit in silence, she started in.

"Look at this one, always with her nose hidden in some book." The other girls laughed, as Ruth sunk a little deeper in her chair. "Bookworm's too good for the likes of us, I guess." Janice packed up her lunch and walked past Ruth, giving her a long hard stare.

I watched the smirk on Janice's face and thought of Edgar's reaction whenever I opened a book. I could never tell if he was upset that I'd chosen a book over spending time with him, or because he struggled with reading and writing and thought I was somehow showing off. He'd left school in the fifth grade and was sensitive about it. Either way, as always, I wanted to keep him happy, so I'd eventually stopped reading.

The bell rang and the rest of the women began to leave the lunchroom. I walked alongside Ruth and asked what book she was reading. She slowly turned the book so I could see the cover: *Jane Eyre*. I smiled back at her and gave a nod to show I knew the book. I could still remember the passage I had memorized for my recital in Boston. Without speaking, she tucked the book into her bag and went back to work.

The next day, I sat with her. I knew Janice would not make rude comments to Ruth with a supervisor sitting next to her. And that's how it went from then on. Ruth was smart and quiet and had been a keen student in school, just like me. Slowly, we became friends. She'd moved to Amherst with her husband, Ken, the new head machinist in the mill. They had no children, and she'd left a job at a library in Cape Breton behind. It was because of her that I went to the Amherst library on that rainy Saturday, when my fog began to lift.

When I entered the library, the first thing I did was close my eyes and take in the comforting smell. The musty, pungent mixture of old paper and ink. I had not realized how much I missed that smell. Someone tapped me on the shoulder and I jumped. I turned, expecting to see Ruth.

"You must be Helen." A tall man smiled down at me. He had blond curly hair and the gentlest, bluest eyes I'd ever seen. "I'm a friend of Ruth's. She asked that I tell you she had to leave." He paused and held his finger in the air like he was trying to remember something very important. "She said she was sorry to miss you, but she knew you would forgive her." He laughed and continued to smile at me. I was at a loss for words. Those blue eyes.

I looked past him to the clock above the librarian's desk. It said four forty-five. I checked my watch. "My watch is wrong." I tapped it with my finger and shook my head. "It stopped."

The librarian cleared her throat and frowned at us. She pointed to the clock. "We close soon. If you want to check out a book, you'll have to do it now."

He laughed. "You look like you could use a cup of coffee. I was just on my way to the diner. Would you join me?" I was still staring at him. "I'm sorry," he extended his hand. "I forgot to introduce myself. I'm Joe. Joe Hingley."

"Helen." I took his hand and shook it. "Helen Campbell." Then, because I was my mother's daughter, I added, "Mrs. Helen Campbell."

He laughed again. "Well, Mrs. Helen Campbell, you're dripping all over the floor and Betsy wants to close the library, so what say we get you to the diner where you can dry off and have a nice hot cup of coffee."

I followed him to the diner. I had the feeling I would have followed him anywhere.

"I don't usually bring strangers here," he said as he opened the door. "It's kind of my home away from home."

Before I could reply, the waitress was in front of us. "Hi, Joe. Usual for you today?"

"Just some coffees thanks, Trudy." Joe steered me to a booth and we sat down. "I can't cook, so I'm pretty well-known here," he said with a smile.

Almost every person in the diner turned to watch us take our seats. "I can see that," I said.

When Trudy brought the coffee, Joe introduced me to her. "This is Helen, I rescued her from a near drowning at the library." She laughed at Joe and left us.

The five young boys at the table next to us strained their necks to get a good look at me.

"You boys mind your manners," Joe said to the table.

"Yes sir, Mr. Hingley," they replied in unison as their heads snapped back.

I couldn't help but laugh.

"I teach English at the school here in town," he said. "It seems everybody knows me."

"Except me." I folded my hands in front of me on the table and looked at him expectantly. He laughed and took up the challenge. He told me he was a baseball player in his younger days. He was obsessed with the Yankees. He loved Shakespeare. He had never married. He coached a boys' baseball team. He read novels constantly. He had asthma. He was an only child. He always had peppermints in his pocket. He grew up in a small town in New Brunswick where everyone farmed potatoes. His parents were both dead. He went to the library just about every day, and that is where he'd met Ruth. He did not smoke. Lemon pie was his favourite, and he went to the pictures every chance he got.

What he didn't say was that his laugh was like medicine, that his eyes smiled constantly, and that he had a radiating kindness most people could never hope to attain.

And what did I tell him of Helen Campbell that first rainy day in April? More than I ever dreamed I would. I told him I had one sister and one brother. I'd lost my father when I was fifteen. I wanted to be a teacher as well, but left school to work at the mill and help my mother. I was married to a man who was overseas. I worked in Halifax for a year and then moved here to take a supervisor's position. I had a friend named Madge. Today was my first day in the library. I was from Truro. I had not gone to the pictures in over a year. I liked apple pie. I had not read a book in over four years. I'd recently met Ruth and she was my only friend in Amherst. I worked overtime whenever I could. I had not been out to a dance in almost three years. I loved the smell of the library. I rented a room from an old lady with whom I rarely spoke. I didn't know anything about the Yankees. I'd lived in Boston when I was younger. I loved to skate. This was my first time at the diner.

"I've talked too much," I said after our second cup of coffee. "What are you reading?" I pointed to the book he had brought from the library.

"It's poetry. One of my favourites. Do you want to hear some?"

I was suddenly shy, imagining him reading poetry to me in the middle of the diner, but I couldn't resist that smile, or those eyes. He looked so earnest. I nodded.

He opened the book to a page he had marked with a piece of green string.

Two roads diverged in a yellow wood,
And sorry I could not travel both
And be one traveler, long I stood
And looked down one as far as I could
To where it bent in the undergrowth;

Then took the other, as just as fair,
And having perhaps the better claim,
Because it was grassy and wanted wear;
Though as for that the passing there
Had worn them really about the same,

And both that morning equally lay
In leaves no step had trodden black.
Oh, I kept the first for another day!
Yet knowing how way leads on to way,
I doubted if I should ever come back.

I shall be telling this with a sigh
Somewhere ages and ages hence:
Two roads diverged in a wood, and I–
I took the one less traveled by,
And that has made all the difference.

As he read, I could see the pure joy on his face. I was mesmerized. Who was this man, and where had he come from?

"That was written by Robert Frost." He smiled and closed the book. "I don't want to bore you to death on the very day I rescued you from drowning."

"I liked it very much," I said.

"Do you have a favourite book?" he asked.

"Yes." I twirled my coffee cup on the table as I spoke. "*Jane Eyre.*"

He smiled and leaned across the booth. His voice just above a whisper: *"I am no bird, and no net ensnares me. I am a free human being with an independent will."*

I found it hard to contain my growing grin. "Very good, professor," I said.

By the time we finished our coffees, it felt like I had known Joe Hingley my entire life. And he seemed, already, to know me. "You're a living ghost," he said as I left the diner that first day. "All work and no play. We need to get you back out in the world."

And that is just what he did.

Joe became my second friend in Amherst, and the library was our common ground. We read, talked about books, went for walks, and always ended our outing with a coffee at the diner. He never asked about Edgar and I never offered. Sometimes Ruth joined us, but mostly it was just the two of us. I couldn't help but wonder if she'd not shown up that day at the library on purpose. We never held hands, we never kissed, we just enjoyed each other's company. I was a married woman, after all. He could only be my friend. I took nothing from him, except peppermints and books.

When I wasn't with him, I could still hear his laugh, like it was buried deep in my pocket. He brought joy to my life and he could see that it was a surprise to me every time I smiled. "You'll get used to it," he laughed. He was so wise. He knew me before I knew myself.

One day at the diner, when I was returning from the ladies' room, I overheard two of the waitresses talking. "I hope this one works out for the poor professor," one said. They stopped speaking when they saw me. Like Truro, I knew this was a place where secrets were traded and people were discussed as casually as the weather. I decided I didn't care. Joe was my friend, and I wasn't going to give up this bit of happiness I had found.

The Uniform

When I left Halifax, I wrote Edgar. Aunt Gertie warned me to hold off on the letter. She wanted me to keep getting the money from the army. But I couldn't wait. It felt wrong to let Edgar think I would be waiting for him when he returned. Being in Amherst with so many soldiers kept him on my mind and the letter was my first small step toward setting myself free. I wrote that I didn't think we would be able to stay together after the war. I didn't go into much detail. I said that there had been too many lies, too much pain and sadness. I couldn't bring myself to mention the many months of syphilis treatments and the unforgivable humiliation I had endured. I told him I was living in Amherst and that I hoped he was safe.

He never wrote back. But the money stopped coming soon after. I knew Edgar's temper. I knew he would stop the payments. I didn't care. I now made enough money to get by on my own, and when I finally began to find some happiness, the worry of Edgar's presence in my life no longer weighed me down. I thought it would be as simple as signing a paper when he returned, and then we would both go our separate ways. The only real obstacle I could imagine was my mother. She had been frantic when I told her about the letter. Of course, she didn't know about the syphilis, the treatments, the extent of Edgar's violence, or my crushing unhappiness. Even if she knew, I was sure she would still be on his side.

I went back to Truro for a visit a few months after I met Joe. Aunt Gertie and I had been exchanging letters. She had been under the weather and I wanted to see her. I did not tell anyone about Joe, but as soon as Aunt Gertie saw me, she knew. She knew I was happy and that there was probably a man responsible for it. She smiled from her bed. "There's the girl I know," she said. I leaned in for a hug.

"You're so thin. Are you sicker than you let on? What does the doctor—"

"Don't you worry about me," she cut me off. "I'll be just fine. Now, make us some tea and tell me about whoever brought your smile back."

I told her about Ruth, about Joe, about the library and how happy I was. "You can't tell anyone though," I said. "I need this to be mine for now. We really are just friends, but I want Joe to be something just for me, if that makes sense."

"My lips are sealed. Maybe for the first time ever." She took my hand. "I knew you would find love again, Helen. Hold on to it, hold on tight."

My mother arrived just then with some groceries. She, too, could sense something had changed, but she immediately came to her own conclusions. "Just remember you're a married woman, Helen. I don't want to hear any gossip coming through those squawking women at the mill about your goings-on in Amherst. You have a husband, and he'll be coming home when this war is over. You'll need to stand by him. Imagine what he's been through. He's going to need us."

"I don't want to discuss this, Mother. I came here to visit Aunt Gertie." I got off the bed and took a step toward her. "But I do think you'd better get used to the idea that I will not be married to Edgar once the war is over."

I leaned down to kiss Aunt Gertie goodbye and walked out the door.

My heart pounded the entire walk to the train station. I didn't dare look behind me. I thought I might see my mother running after me, screaming for me to do as she says. I repeated what I had said to her over and over in my head. I couldn't stop smiling. It was a wonderful feeling.

I was content with my life in Amherst and I didn't want my old life in Truro to ruin my happiness. Ruth and I had become close friends and we spent time together with Joe and Ken, or just the two of us, walking the quiet roads beyond town. My fog had lifted, and I could finally see a new future ahead. Sometimes I imagined that future with Joe. We had such a wonderful time when we were together. We spent hours in the library, just reading, not speaking more than a few words to each other. It felt like we were so close in those quiet times.

I never spoke of Edgar to Ruth or Joe and they never asked about him. When we first met, Ruth asked me why I didn't wear a wedding ring. I told her the truth, that I'd given it to Edgar when he went overseas. Now, after so many months had passed without my speaking of him, I just assumed they knew I did not have a happy marriage.

It never occurred to me that someone might think I'd taken my ring off to appear unwed. Not until I went to a dance with Ruth and her husband.

At first, I said I couldn't go. I didn't want to be around soldiers. But Ruth said this wasn't like the YMCA dance, it was run by the rotary club and there wouldn't be many soldiers. So, I went. There were only two uniforms in the room. I danced with Ken twice and declined requests from both soldiers. I noticed later that one of them was dancing with Janice Walker's cousin, Minnie, who also worked at the mill.

Joe showed up halfway through the evening and I was surprised, but happy, to see him there. "You've finally broken your spell and come out to a dance." He laughed and extended his hand. As he led me to the dance floor, I realized this was the first time we'd touched, since the day we shook hands. When he took me in his arms, I knew we were more than friends. As the music played and the other couples moved around us, I could only feel his arms around me. I felt instantly relaxed and overcome with joy as I let myself be drawn in closer. He looked at me like I was the only person in the room, and I knew. These were not the same feelings I had once had with Edgar. This was new, a feeling just for him. Those blue eyes made me feel safe.

After a few songs, we went back to sit with Ruth and Ken. As soon as I sat down, one of the soldiers approached our table. "Now that you're warmed up," he slurred, bumping the back of my chair, "maybe you'd like to give me a try." He held his hand out to me.

It was the uniform that reminded me so much of Edgar. The same khaki brown slacks, the same shirt and tie. Just looking at him made me nervous. "No thank you, I'm happy here with my friends for now." I gave him a weak smile and turned back to Joe.

"Well, you see, my new friends over there thought you might be Helen Campbell, little Eddie Campbell's wife, that lousy coward." He paused as if he might spit on the floor at the mention of Edgar's name. "But I don't see a ring on that finger, and I see you here with the professor, so maybe my buddy's got it all wrong. Maybe you're not married to that stinking coward, and you'd like to dance with me?"

I felt the same heavy fear move over my body that I used to feel when Edgar was drinking. An electric vibration in the air that signalled the threat of violence. My hands started to shake. I went to stand, and Joe gently put his hand on my shoulder. He stood and glared down at the soldier, who now looked like a young boy dressed up to play war. Joe was a good six inches taller than him.

"The lady said no thank you."

I heard the scrape of another chair. Ken now stood on the other side of the soldier, who shook his head and looked up at the two large men. He seemed to sober up before our eyes. He muttered his apologies and walked away.

I looked at Ruth. "How would he know anything about me?"

"This is a small place, Helen." She put her hand on mine. "I'm sure they think they know everything about all of us. I don't want you to worry about it."

"Why don't I take you home?" Joe smiled down at me and handed me my coat. This would be the first time he ever walked me home. We normally met at the library, or the diner, or at the park for a walk on Sundays. To have him walk me home felt strange, especially after what had just happened. I took his arm and we left.

We walked in silence, but it was not the same easy silence we normally shared. When we reached my place, I thanked him for bringing me home.

"Do you know one of the reasons I like books so much, Helen?" He looked so serious, yet he still smiled. "Because when the people in the story disappoint me, I can simply close the book and move on." He reached for my hand and held it to his chest. "You're the first person I have met who I know could never, and would never, disappoint me." He let go of my hand and continued down the street. "I'll see you at the library," he called out before he turned the corner.

I couldn't sleep that night. There were so many things running through my mind. But there was one word I couldn't get out of my head. The soldier had said it twice.

Coward.

Apple Pie

Fall 1944

"We had it out again." I sat at the table and twisted my hand-kerchief in my hands. "She took the train to Amherst, just to see me. She insists I go back to Edgar when he returns. She won't hear of me divorcing him and making a new life for myself. All she talks about is *commitment* and *honouring our vows*. It doesn't seem to matter that Edgar has honoured nothing. I think all she cares about is what people will say, what they'll think of a woman who gets a divorce—or more likely, that woman's mother!"

Aunt Gertie took a pie out of the oven and set it on the sideboard. The cool air from the window filled the room with the sweetness of apples and cinnamon. She said nothing as she picked up a tea towel and started to dry her dishes

"What is the secret between my mother and father? I know they were married in Boston." She dropped the bowl she was drying in the sink and turned to me. "Not all secrets are buried, Aunt Gertie. I saw a picture of their wedding day at Aunt Nettie's. It was taken in front of Uncle Pat's shop. Why is that a secret? Why is so much of her life hidden?"

She sat at the kitchen table opposite me. Her hair was not styled and she wore no makeup. Her apron wore her morning's baking, and I could see her dress was loose on her. Her last letter had said she was feeling better, but I still worried about her. Her eyes were tired, and she moved slowly. I looked down at her wrinkled hands as she ran them along the tablecloth, smoothing it out and gathering her thoughts. There was no denying it. She was getting old.

"Your mother would never want you to know this story. She would say it was her story, and hers only, to tell," Aunt Gertie began. "But she'll never tell it. She'll take it to her grave." She looked up at me to see if I understood. I nodded and she continued.

"Daughters don't see their mothers as anything but that, mothers. But they were all young once. And when your mother was young, she loved a man just as desperately as you first loved Edgar. In fact, they were engaged to be married. She was happy back then, full of life and mischief. I know you find that hard to believe, but she was. Just a young girl with her whole life ahead of her. But as often happens, the plans of the young are made in foolish haste. Her beau was a friend of your father's, Robert. There was a crowd of them that all went to the dances.

"One night, Blanche was out with Robert and Jim and another couple. On the drive home, your father went off the road at the Valley Bridge. He'd been drinking, your father. Robert was thrown from the car and into the river. The spring thaw made the ice soft and he went right through. It was dark and they couldn't see anything, couldn't see him. Your father tried to find him. Almost killed himself trying. But he couldn't do it. Your mother had a nasty cut on her neck, but she was okay. Everyone else survived.

"Jim was very shook up. Robert was his best friend. Without a word to anyone, he left the next week and boarded a boat for Boston. Your mother was devastated." Gertie shook her head at the memory, paused, and took a deep breath before she continued. "Then she found out she was pregnant, only a few weeks after he was gone."

Our eyes met across the table and she was silent for almost a minute. "They would have been married by then, but now she was on her own and had nowhere to turn. She took the boat to Boston and found your father. She knew where he'd be, with Nettie. She told him her news and said he was coming home with her to raise the child. She'd never liked him and she sure as shootin' didn't want to marry him. But in her mind, she had no other choice. He didn't hesitate. They were married the next day and went home to Nova Scotia that week."

The scar. I could see it so clearly. Whenever she was worried or sitting alone lost in her thoughts, my mother's hand would go to that scar. I'd never given it much thought, but now that I knew the truth, I could see her running her finger along it, below her right ear, over and over. I had a feeling of pity for her then that I hadn't known I was capable of. And then another memory flashed in my mind. I remembered my father skating at the Boston Commons, his beautiful eyes shadowed in darkness as he told me about Robert, the boy who could skate so fast.

I looked at Aunt Gertie, and the pain I felt when my father died once again took hold of my heart. "Their lives could have been so different."

"We each have our journey, Helen, and very rarely is it a straight line. Your father did all he could for your mother. And I think he even came to love her. I know he tried. She just wasn't capable of loving him."

"You're right," I said. "She wasn't capable of loving the daughter who reminded her of him, either." I remembered the loving way she used to stare at Russell. "She loved Russell more than anyone. You could see it every time she looked at him. Even Eunie didn't get that kind of love."

They were bitter words. Words I'd carried from my childhood but never spoken. I didn't mean to sound cruel, or angry, yet as soon as I spoke, I was surprised at how close to the surface these feelings truly were. I knew it wasn't Russell's fault how my mother chose to love her children. But so much finally made sense.

I was still twisting my handkerchief. Gertie took it from me and gently placed her hands around mine. "It's okay, love," she said. "We all wear our past. It's impossible to shed."

Black Crows

Fall 1945

Jennie walked toward me, avoiding the bins and wooden crates lining the isles between sewing machines. I thought one of the girls must be needed at home. It was rare for anybody from the office to be on the production floor.

"Helen, you're wanted in the office." She met my eyes for only an instant, then concentrated on the floor.

"What is it?" I asked.

"Family business, I think. Your mother is here."

Aunt Gertie. She was my first thought. I rushed down the corridor. The door to the head manager's office was open and I could see my mother sitting in a chair, her back to me. I rushed in, ignoring Mr. Parks sitting at his desk. "Is it Aunt Gertie? What's happened?"

"It's not Gertie." Her head turned slightly, but I still couldn't see her face. Her voice was firm but held an unfamiliar edge. Fear, maybe? I couldn't tell. "Your husband is home. You need to come back."

Her words hung in the air like a lone rifle shot in the deep winter woods.

I reached for the back of the chair in front of me. With my hands shaking, I lowered myself and sat facing Mr. Parks. Two crows perched motionless on the bare oak branches outside his window. They watched me in silence, their black bodies stark against the grey November sky. I sensed my life slipping away.

"Your mother's filled me in, Helen. I want to help in any way I can. She brought this letter from the Truro mill." He held up the evidence and waved it before me. "They're happy to find a spot for you again. These are difficult times for many families." His voice cracked slightly and he cleared his throat. "As our men come home." His bald head was beginning to shine with sweat and he continued to hold the letter and stare at his desk. "I know your mother has been such a help to you, Helen, what with getting you the job here at our mill, and now in returning to Truro. You are lucky to have her."

His last words brought me back to the room. How had my mother helped me to get this job? How much had she been doing that I didn't know about? I turned to her, a question about to escape my lips. She reached over and squeezed my hand. When was the last time she'd touched me?

"Thank you, Mr. Parks." My mother rose and looked down at me. "Mr. Parks and I think it best that you come home today, Helen. Go get your things and I'll wait for you at the main door." She pulled her gloves on slowly. She was standing straight as a rod, her chest pushed out, her chin raised slightly. She was ready for anything.

I followed her into the hall. She turned and cut me off before I could speak. "Don't make this harder than it already is. Don't make a scene."

Once outside, I could see Edgar's brother Lincoln sitting in the driver's seat of an old rusted Buick. He watched us approach with little interest as he smoked his cigarette.

The car rocked back and forth as it manoeuvred the frozen muddy ruts on our way through town. The November cold crept through the seat and seeped into my legs. I felt numb. We passed the diner, and I lowered my head.

"Where is he?" I surprised myself with the sound of my voice, a rough whisper. "You can't make me go back." I turned to her and I knew I sounded weak. I could feel the courage I'd built up over the last year draining from my body. I was terrified of what this woman could make me do.

"It's for the best." My mother kept her eyes straight ahead, as if she were driving. "You'll see. You need to be with Edgar now."

When we reached my street, I saw my landlady on the front porch, wrapped in an old shawl. She nodded at my mother as we went up the steps. They looked like two old friends, conspiring in the war effort, trying to trap the enemy.

"You go in." My mother opened the door for me. "I'll settle things with Mrs. MacDonald."

An old familiar smell filled the room. Aqua Velva. For a fleeting moment, it took me back to a happier time, my head nestled in my husband's neck, his arms around me. But I kept my eyes on the floor, locked on the faded carpet, unsure if I would be able to look up, look into his eyes.

"Hello, Helen." His voice was soft, different. I slowly lifted my eyes. He stood beside the chair, a cane in his right hand. He leaned on it for support, and I could tell from his grip that it was taking great effort to remain standing. I'd expected to see him in uniform, but he wore his old clothes. His pants hung off him and his shirt looked two sizes too big. He wore a red tie and no hat. His face was thin and clean-shaven. He was the same, but different. He smiled, that same crooked smile, and took a step toward me.

"What happened? Have you hurt your leg?" I felt like I was floating, watching the scene unfold like a picture show. And then I realized, that was exactly it: it was a picture, the one I had seen as a kid, the soldier returning from war. I was having a hard time believing this was real, that Edgar Campbell was actually standing in front of me. He put his arm out, inviting me closer.

"Don't." I moved aside and walked past him. My mother came into the room and held his arm as he slid into a chair.

"Edgar's lost both his legs, Helen." She threw the words at me. Her face was twisted in anger and spite. She looked at me as if I had been the one to cut his legs off and was still holding the saw.

I dropped to a kitchen chair and looked at his legs. A small whimper escaped my lips before I could stop it. I recognized that sound. It was the same small cry I had made the day I heard my father was dead. Hearing it again now made me realize it was for my loss, not his, just as it had been all those years ago. The fabric of Edgar's pants rested on the unnatural curve at his knees. I had no words. He took the cane and tapped his leg, and a hollow sound echoed through the room.

"I've got a wooden set now." A bitter grin spread across his face. "Courtesy of the Krauts."

I packed my things and Lincoln took them to the car. He helped Edgar down the stairs. They looked like one giant beast, arms intertwined, a mixture of moving parts and futile appendages. My mother found me sitting on the edge of my bed, running my hands over the cover of my library book. "Whoever he is, you'll need to forget him now." She took the book from me and left it on the bedside table. "You're done here." The small piece of green string curled its way outside the pages of the book, marking where I had been.

I sat in the back seat with my mother. I could feel that old familiar fog closing in on me as we made our way down the highway. I felt like I was drowning in it, sinking from sight with every passing moment. I wondered what would be left of me by the time we reached Truro.

When we arrived, I discovered Edgar and my mother already had a place rented for us on Mill Street. I could only wonder how much had been kept from me. How much of my life had been controlled by my mother. The cupboard was stocked with food and Mother had put fresh flowers on the table. White carnations. I threw them in the garbage the moment she left.

Woollen Stockings
& Baby Powder

W e were like intimate strangers. He didn't talk about the war and I didn't ask. He didn't ask about the treatments I'd endured, my life in Halifax, or my time in Amherst, and I didn't talk about it. He didn't give me my wedding ring back, and I didn't ask if he still had it. He acted as if nothing had passed between us. He looked at me with such hope and adoration, like he had never read the letter I sent him. For Edgar, it was as if we'd picked up where we left off, except he was now a sober cripple and I was the only light in his day.

"The best of us can rise to any occasion." How many times had I heard Uncle Pat say this during my time in Boston? I'd never given the phrase, or his enduring optimism, much thought. Now, I thought I could finally understand what he meant. But rising wasn't easy, and I didn't think I was among the best of us. The simple fact was, the more I rose, the farther I fell.

The daily routine of Edgar's care did not improve as the weeks passed. Applying the ointment to his wrinkled, scarred wounds; willing my hands to touch him, to clean him, to care for him. Trying not to gag from the putrid odours and his dry, flaking flesh. I can still feel the rough texture of the woollen stockings in my hands as I pulled them over his rounded stumps. How the straps strained against his upper thighs, creating deep indentations by the end of the day. More ointment would need to be applied to those lines of red, raw skin when I reversed the process before bedtime and removed the stockings. It was hateful.

He was able to pull on the prosthetic legs himself. The metal hinges and straps were a constant source of pain, leaving deep bruises and carving raw sores into his flesh. He never complained. We both got through it, each with our own silent strength, pulled from unknown depths. He begged me to hold him, to kiss him, to climb on top of him and let him be a man again. And I did it. I cried afterward, silent tears he couldn't see. Sometimes he cried, too. It was hard to see a man so reduced, so utterly lost and dejected. Through it all, we never spoke of the past. We never spoke of the sorrow that hung in the air. When he woke in a cold sweat—"My legs are on fire!"—grabbing for the limbs he no longer had, I held him and let him cry on my breast.

My mother fussed over Edgar, made his favourite meals and sat with him for hours. She pulled me aside one evening after dinner. "Has he ever mentioned Gerald or any of the other North Novas?" Her voice was so low I could hardly make her out.

"He doesn't talk about the war," I said.

"Just as well." She grabbed a tea towel and started to dry my dishes. "I saw Gerald Johnson's mother today. She didn't ask about Edgar, and I didn't mention he was home. I think people just want to keep to themselves and forget. She seems lonely. Says she's going to start taking in boarders." I was surprised my mother mentioned any of this, but I too had thought it odd Edgar hadn't mentioned anyone from the war, not even Gerald or Madge.

I spoke of Madge once when Edgar and I first went back to Truro. "I think I'll walk out to see Mrs. Somers today. See if she knows where Madge is living now," I said.

Edgar's voice rose for the first time since he'd been back. "I can't have you going all the way out there." He grabbed his thigh and winced. "I'm in terrible pain today and I want you to stay with me. You are gone most days and I just want you with me on the weekend—is that too much to ask?"

So I stayed home. When thoughts of Joe consumed me, I did my best to shut them out. I could not bear to think of him, of how he'd told me I could never disappoint him.

I continued to wonder where Madge could be living. I'd heard about Gerald's passing the past summer when I was living in Amherst. Aunt Gertie wrote to tell me. I cried and cried when I read that letter. I cried for the good man Gerald had been and the life he would never have, the children he'd never had, and now never would. I wrote to Madge, but my letter was returned in the mail. I thought I might have the wrong address, so I wrote to Mrs. Somers, but I never heard back from her either. In the end I sent a note of condolence to Mrs. Johnson. She sent me back a lovely thank you. I felt deeply sorry for her, first a widow and then to lose her only child. I tried to remind myself that I wasn't the only person suffering.

I found it hard to have any kind of conversation with Edgar. I was still living on tiptoe, as I had in the past, worried he could have an outburst at any moment. But I needed to know about his army wages.

"I'm worried about money," I said one evening. "My wages aren't enough. We need the army money to get by. Do you know when it'll come?"

He was in his chair, where he normally spent his day. His wooden legs were next to him, leaning against the table. "That's the government for you. They're always mixing things up." He rubbed the top of his thighs, a habit he maintained even though his left leg was now gone above the knee and his right ended just below. "Don't you worry." He looked up and smiled at me. "I'll look into it. We'll be fine. I promise."

It was such a surprise to me that Edgar could even smile given what he had been through. I couldn't begin to imagine the horrors he'd seen in the war and what circumstances might have led to his legs being amputated. I never asked. He had suffered enough.

I did write a letter to the Army Office on my own, inquiring about Edgar's pay. Though I pitied him, his promises were still hollow. I had no faith he would look into his pay. I didn't tell him about the letter. I figured they would simply find the error and the payments would start again. We couldn't go on the way we were, with me working every extra shift I could just to keep food on the table.

They were hard days. Days that left me on my knees sobbing into a dishrag so Edgar wouldn't hear me. Maybe it would have been easier if I loved him. "What would I do without you?" He said it every day. I never had an answer. That was in the beginning. I thought I was living through my darkest hours. I didn't think it could get any worse.

I was wrong. By month four, he started to drink again.

My visits with Aunt Gertie were my only escape. Between work and home, it seemed there was no space or time to breathe my own breath. I buried all thoughts of Joe deep inside my heart. I'd left Amherst the way I had gone, like a silent ghost. Joe was now my past.

I finally broke down and cried in Aunt Gertie's arms one Sunday afternoon, after leaving Edgar behind, still sleeping off the drink from the night before. "I don't know why I stay, but what can I do? I don't love him. He's back to his old self, drinking and miserable. Why am I still there?"

She held me just as she had when I was a young girl who'd lost her father. "Guilt is the strongest of all devils," she said. "It can make you do things you never dreamed you were capable of."

Uncle Johnny came in to find me wiping my eyes at the kitchen table. Aunt Gertie was making us a cup of tea. He tossed a bag on the counter and a poof of white powder rose quickly from the top before settling back down. The smell of baby powder instantly filled the kitchen.

"I got the talcum powder, Collie. The kind you like." He took the kettle from her and moved her to a chair at the table. "Don't be tiring yourself out, now." He turned and held my eyes. There was a look of resentment in his stare. He took two teacups from the cupboard and set them between us. "I think it's time, Collie. Time you told her." His lips gently brushed her cheek, and he left the room.

I looked in her eyes and I knew. "You're sick again."

She started to smooth out the tablecloth, her hands moving away from each other, across the fabric, as they had so many times before. I stared at her thin, bony fingers and her sunken cheeks. The skin hung down over her jawbone like it had given up, as if her body was ready to return to the earth.

"Cancer." She lit a cigarette and looked out the window. She took long, deep drags. I followed her gaze and watched the snowflakes · fall outside. "They don't think I'll see the spring."

The tears in my eyes felt heavy, too heavy. I blinked them back and moved to the floor beside her. I buried my head in her lap and she ran her hand over my hair, smoothing it out, just like the tablecloth.

"We're on this earth a short time, love." She put her hand under my chin and raised my face so I could look into her eyes. "For some of us, it's too short." She shed no tears. She looked as brave as she had always seemed. "You'll find your way clear of him some day." She smiled then. "You'll find the strength to live your life, Helen. I know you will. And you won't need me to do it."

Wafts of Whiskey
& Damp Earth

The first time I lost my coupons I blamed myself. The weight of looking after Edgar, with his rages and constant demands, combined with my long hours at work, had me struggling to remember what day it was. Edgar's drinking was out of control. His brother Lincoln was now a permanent fixture in our house, bringing him booze and drinking with him. Edgar continued to find new ways to be cruel when he drank, and lost all of his grateful moments when he was in such a state.

I was exhausted, physically and mentally, just trying to make it through the week. So, I wasn't surprised when I went to glue my coupons that I couldn't find half of them. I figured I'd lost them walking home from work. I didn't bother to tell Edgar. I could only imagine his reaction and the fight that would come of it. I handed my book in that week and made no comment when my supervisor raised her eyebrows and waited for my reply. She knew how much I worked. She knew my book should be full. I said nothing. She was not one to show sympathy and I didn't want to share my troubles. It was hard enough being back on production and having someone else supervise my work. I yearned for my days in Amherst, when I walked the production floor with a confidence that was now a fading memory. I took the loss and moved on. We were still waiting on Edgar's army pay and he kept assuring me it would come through any day. They never replied to my letter, so I didn't know what else I could do.

It was about a month later that I first heard rumours of coupons being sold around town. One of the girls from the office was friends with Rose, who sat at the machine behind me. Rose told me that Mr. Stanfield was looking into some kind of black market that was said to be operating in town, people stealing coupons and selling them to workers.

"Who do they think is stealing our coupons?" I asked.

"That's all I know, Helen," she said. "But it sure seems unfair when we work our hands to the bone all day and someone else is getting the credit, and our money."

As I left work that day, I made sure my coupons were all tucked inside my purse. When I got home, Edgar's chair was empty, as was the bottle of whiskey on the table. He hardly ever left the house, so I didn't know where he could be. All of Rose's talk had me worried about my coupons, so I wanted to get them all sorted out and glued in my book. I went to the cupboard for the tin where I kept my coupon book and the coupons from the week. The tin was gone. I opened every cupboard and drawer. Nothing. My mind began to race. Had someone broken in and stolen the coupons? Was this a coincidence, that I had just learned of this today and now I was somehow a victim? I walked around the small room, trying to figure out what was happening.

That's when I saw the tin under Edgar's chair. It was empty.

It was like a blow to the stomach. He was stealing my coupons. He was stealing from our own house, taking food out of our own mouths, risking eviction from the only place we could afford. I only had one day's worth of coupons in my purse. The rest had been in the tin. If I didn't get the book back, I wouldn't have enough to pay the rent next week.

I was sitting in his chair holding the tin when Edgar came through the door. On his best days he had trouble walking with his prosthetic legs, but when he was drunk it was a sad, pathetic sight that could make me forgive him anything. Not tonight.

As he slid through the door and fell down in a drunken haze, the bottle he was holding rolled across the floor and came to rest at my feet. I let the contents slowly drain around my worn shoes. My long days behind a noisy, vibrating sewing machine were all I could see as I watched the stain grow on the dirty old rug. I was angry, at him and at myself. But it was a weak anger, the kind that drains you of energy and makes you sad. *How could I be so stupid? How could I not have seen this coming?* I looked down at my husband and felt nothing but disgust. My pity was fading, and my affection was long dead. He was passed out on the floor, and just like the many other nights, he would likely piss his pants and sleep where he lay. I searched his pockets to see if he had any coupons left, or any money, but found nothing.

I left early the next the morning. Edgar was still on the floor, snoring. The stench of urine and whiskey hit me as I stepped over him. I was outside Mr. Stanfield's door before his secretary arrived. I didn't want to explain this to my supervisor. I didn't want to be the subject of lunchroom gossip that day. I remembered the day I came to this office with a note from my mother pinned inside my jacket. Here I was again, this time with my own problems.

Mr. Stanfield listened to me and let me tell the entire story. He didn't question me or accuse me in any way of being responsible for any of it. In fact, he simply nodded and took out his handkerchief when it looked like I may start to cry. But I didn't need it. I kept my composure and I told him all I knew. "I understand if you have to let me go," I said.

"I wouldn't hear of it, Helen," he said. "You won't be going anywhere except back down to work." He put the handkerchief back in his pocket and led me to the door. "I don't want you to worry about a thing. Your wages will be covered, and this will stay between you and me. Understand?"

I was speechless. I managed to nod, and thanked him.

"You just take care of yourself, now."

The secretaries had their eyes lowered, tapping on their typewriters, when I left. I thought I might see Eunie there, but luckily I didn't. I could not bring myself to share this story with her.

I went back downstairs and was behind my machine before the starting bell rang. I was glad to be there, to be busy. It was impossible to think about Edgar when I had to concentrate on my sewing.

On my way back from the lunchroom I saw the line supervisor speaking to an elderly lady and a young man. I recognized her immediately: Mrs. Parsons. I put my head down as I passed them, but she stepped slightly to the side to stop my progress.

"Hello, Helen." She smiled and surveyed me from head to toe. No doubt taking in my sewing apron, my worn shoes, and my tired eyes. She explained she had brought her nephew Alistair in to apply for a job. Alistair and the line supervisor moved along the hall toward the office and Mrs. Parsons remained firm-footed in front of me. Before she could attack with her first question, I blurted my own out.

"Have you heard of Madge lately, Mrs. Parsons? I haven't had word from her in years."

"Oh, Helen. She's in a bad state, that one. Home for good now, with her old crippled-up mother looking after her. The father, he died years ago, as you know. A stroke. And the son, well, he died in the war of course and that just about killed Mrs. Somers, it truly did. That poor woman. And now with the girl home, I don't know how Mrs. Somers is going to manage."

"Is Madge ill?" I asked.

"Oh, child, you don't know, of course you don't. They won't tell anyone about her." She leaned closer to me and whispered in my ear. "It was a car accident. Happened about two years ago now. What a tragedy it was. I think she wishes she was one of those who didn't survive. You know? Three others died, two other gals and a young fellow, all from Halifax. Just Madge and the other fellow survived. We never found out for sure who he was, though." She paused and searched my face for a moment. "She won't talk about it. I was up visiting my relatives in New Brunswick at the time, you see. So, I didn't get it fresh, all that happened. I just got the settling dust."

Mrs. Parsons's face faded as my heart began pounding. It was like a freight train in my chest. It pounded and pounded as she continued the story.

"Her face is such a mess now, all disfigured, and she lost an eye. Poor thing was in the hospital for months. They even sent her to Boston to see what could be done. She was so pretty. You remember, don't you? She was just so pretty. No one could resist those blue eyes. But I tell her, she must look to the bright side. She's alive. And she can walk. I heard the poor other bugger lost both his legs. God only knows what's become of him. She won't talk about it, though. She won't talk about anything, and she won't let anyone come to the house either."

The bell rang to mark the end of lunch, but I heard a blaring train whistle, just as loud as it was years ago the day my father died. It shook my entire body. The weight on my chest was too heavy to bear and my knees buckled beneath me. The next thing I knew I was on my front steps, drenched through from the rain and shivering uncontrollably.

My father always said he saw red when he was angry. But all I could see was a blinding white. When I walked in the room, Edgar was sitting in his chair holding the crystal decanter. He was pouring a drink in the glass he held. I could smell the whiskey from the door. His two wooden legs were propped up against the side table next to his chair. At first, he looked at me with concern. Here I was, home from work hours early, soaked through to the bone, no coat, no hat, and still wearing my sewing apron. But then he must have seen the rage smouldering in my eyes. His own eyes widened and a look of confusion came over him, like a young boy trying to figure out which lie he'd been caught at.

In two strides I was across the room and had one of the wooden legs in my hand. Before he knew what was happening, I struck him across the face with the leg, one of the metal hinges catching his brow and leaving a gash on his head. His glass went flying and smashed to pieces as it hit the floor, the decanter still gripped in his left hand. I was surprised and exhilarated all at once. Like swinging a baseball bat in my younger years, it just seemed like a natural thing to do.

Before he could recover from the first blow, I swung again. I grabbed the other leg and ran to the cellar door just opposite his chair. He watched me with more shock than anger. I raised the two legs, one in each hand, above my head like a triumphant soldier raising a flag and I hurled them down the cellar steps with all my strength. I kept my eyes on his. He now had two good-sized slashes on his left temple and the decanter had broken into large shards which lay in his lap, its contents emptied in his crotch. If he moved, he would cut himself.

The legs clattered as they made their way down the wooden steps and landed on the dirt floor. A distinct, pungent odour rose from the darkness and I was immediately transported to a night long ago, when I sat huddled under another set of steps, hiding from him and fearing a drunken beating. How many times had he hit me? Hit me with his hate, his rage, and his disappointment. He'd hit me with more than his fists, I just didn't realize it then. No good or kindness would ever come from this man. Liquor or no liquor, he was broken.

I was breathing heavy and shaking so hard that my hand was hitting the wall next to me. The rapid tapping of my knuckles echoed throughout the room, like some kind of Morse-code warning.

"Get me my legs, you miserable bitch." Spit flew from his mouth and a familiar anger filled his eyes. "I'll fucking kill you this time."

I wrapped both my hands around the handle and slowly shut the cellar door. I turned, walked past him, and out the front door. His screaming voice faded the farther I walked away. I instinctively put my hand to my belly.

Two of us left that day. Edgar didn't know it, but I did.

Hair Ribbons & Daisies

Summer 1946

I lost Aunt Gertie in June. She faded away, right before our eyes. Uncle Johnny said it was the quietest thing she ever did. I was devastated. Her death brought a void to my life that felt like a physical wound, an aching hole in my chest. The baby inside me was the only thing that kept me going, the only thing that kept that wound from destroying me entirely.

We all felt the loss. I stood with my mother and Eunie as we laid Aunt Gertie to rest. Mother and I had barely spoken since I'd left Edgar. She couldn't understand why I'd done it. I didn't tell her the entire story. I had no doubt someone would eagerly whisper the truth to her someday. But it wouldn't be me. She was mourning now, too. Gertie was her only friend, the only woman I had ever seen her smile with, laugh with, and, in the end, cry with.

It was only the four of us gathered at the cemetery that day, and my large stomach stood out against my slight frame. Grief had not helped my appetite over these past few weeks.

My mother pulled me aside after the service. "Come back and live with us. Let us help you when the baby comes. You don't look well. You should be with family."

"We'll be fine," I said.

"With no father for the child?" she hissed in my ear.

Eunie gave me a weak smile. She was glued to my mother's side as usual. To think I used to envy her when I was a child. I pitied her now. She would never get away. I ignored my mother's words and went to hug Johnny goodbye.

"She was over the moon about the baby," he said. "Collie said you'll make a wonderful mother. I think so too." His voice trailed off and turned to a whisper. "We couldn't have any, you know. Children." He shook his head a little and smiled at me. A kind, sad smile. In his grief, I could see he was still worrying over me. He knew the entire story.

"Thank you, Uncle Johnny." I hugged him tight.

Just before Aunt Gertie passed, Johnny had a friend in the Army Office look into Edgar's pay. He found out Edgar had been dishonourably discharged from the army sometime in 1942. This explained why the money had stopped coming when I was in Amherst. And I now knew Edgar had never received the letter I wrote him. I had pictured him losing his legs on the beaches of Normandy or in the town of Authie, but as it turned out, those places were as foreign to him as they were to me.

I stayed at work until I began to really show. I kept my head held high, but the shame, anger, and resentment I carried weighed on me. If there were whispers among the women at the Mill, they never reached my ears. Mrs. Johnson and Aunt Gertie kept me positive during my pregnancy. Their enthusiasm over the baby brought me strength. Aunt Gertie's last words would linger with me always: "You'll be just fine, Helen. Your road is clear now, and this baby will be your path to joy. Mark my words, you will be so happy."

As always, she knew my thoughts. She knew that I mourned the loss of Madge's friendship. But she wouldn't let me wallow in sorrows which could not be changed. True to her form, she put it as plainly as she ever had, and gave me one last piece of insight before her death. "There's something drawing those two together and God alone knows what it is," she said. "It's got to be a darkness that they share; some kind of misery they were born into."

Aunt Gertie once told me I would love again. She was right. She was right about so many things. Nothing could have prepared me for the love I felt for my baby. She was pure joy, and it was the greatest pleasure of my life to discover that joy in her every breath. I named her Colleen. The moment she was born, I knew I was on a new path.

But even the joy of motherhood could not extinguish the resentment and anger simmering deep in my belly. I set it against Edgar, Madge, and my mother. I reserved the most for myself, however, for my complete naïvité.

After Colleen came, I didn't want to see anyone. It felt like the entire town knew my story, knew what a fool I had been. Even as I held my greatest joy in my arms, I could not shake the feeling of betrayal.

I put Colleen down for her nap one morning, and Mrs. Johnson called me into her room.

"There's something I want to share with you, Helen," she said, handing me a letter. I recognized the writing immediately. It was addressed to Gerald. I looked at her. "It's okay," she said. "Just read it."

I opened the envelope and a faint hint of Madge's lilac perfume escaped.

Dear Gerald–

Your mother told me about your injuries. Words really can't tell you how sorry I am

In my coward's way, I now feel I can be honest with you. I have not always been the best person, and certainly not the wife you deserved, but I need to tell you the truth about the child you mourn. I need to confess, and I hope this will give you some peace.

I don't want your forgiveness because I don't deserve it. I want to help you understand and bring an end to any guilt and pain you carry. The baby I lost was not your child. I knew I was pregnant when I took you to the barn that night. I had to make you think the baby was yours so that you would marry me and get me away from that house. I am sorry.

There is nobody else who knows this. I have never told another soul, and never will. The child was my brother's. He was an evil person and he hurt me in many ways. He always told me he would kill my entire family–burn us in our sleep–if I told anyone what he'd done to me. I believed him. I knew he would do it.

That is why I had no grief for that baby, and in truth, I was glad it did not survive. I prayed for it to die, and I can tell you honestly, I feel no shame in that. I do feel great shame and regret at how I treated you. I have made many mistakes and hurt many people over the years. You are a kind man who deserved so much more. I wish things could have been different. I wish you could have married someone like Helen. You both would have been better off.

I am sorry.

Madge

It was like the answer to a question you never knew existed. These words, like ghosts of the past, carried their pain to the present. I felt an emptiness as the anger I'd held for so long, and with such strength, withered and faded away. It was replaced by grief. Grief for the lost childhood Madge never had and the young woman she never had the chance to become. Aunt Gertie's words came to me again: "*There's something drawing those two together...some kind of misery they were born into.*"

"He never read it." Mrs. Johnson took the letter gently from my hands and put it back in the envelope. "Gerald listed me as his next of kin, not Madge. When the army sent me his things I found this letter, still sealed. It must have arrived after he died." She took my hand. Her eyes were sad, yet she smiled. "He never knew the truth," she said. "He didn't need to, Helen, but you did."

That night I wrote my own letter. I poured my forgiveness onto the page and hoped Madge would accept it and forgive me too. As I looked back through the eyes of a grown woman, and not a naïve child, my memories now made sense. When I finished the letter, I went to my dresser drawer and pulled out the stack I had carried with me all these years. The letters my father sent from Boston when I was a child were tied in the satin hair ribbon Madge gave me the day I told her I was moving to Boston. I wrapped my letter to her in the ribbon and placed it in an envelope.

I thought about Edgar and all that he had been through in his life. It was too painful to imagine forgiving him at that point. I didn't even know where he was. The last I heard he and Lincoln had moved to Toronto, where Lincoln had a job waiting for him. I knew the day would come when I would need to forgive him, too, for Colleen's sake and my own. But that day was years away.

That night I lay in bed and thought about the people I had loved over my life and how I had always believed love and power to be two separate things. But they're not. They can be the same. Hate, too. Madge knew this better than anyone. She knew the struggle. My father had power over me because of his strong love. It blinded me to his faults. My mother had a power over me too, maybe even a stronger power, but it wasn't her love that kept me under control; it was my need for her love, her acceptance. Even back when we were young, Madge had such power over me. She knew I'd do almost anything for her. Almost.

And then there was the power Edgar held over me. First with the promise of love, then with his physical abuse, and in the end, with the grinding force of guilt. At the time I thought nothing could have more power over me than he did, this man I both loved and hated. It proved stronger than a new love, but not stronger than a mother's. That, I knew now, was the ultimate power, the one that would set me free and let me learn to love, and forgive.

The next morning I put Colleen in her pram and set off for the post office. When we reached the corner of Millers Diversion, I noticed a clump of daisies growing along the ditch. It was late in the summer for daisies, but here they were, as bright and cheerful as ever. I could see Madge as she was when we were young, making daisy chains for our hair. She was pure sunshine back then.

I picked a handful of daisies and turned the pram around. I headed back toward Madge's house. There had been too many letters in my life. Too many second-hand words. I was going to tell Madge my words in person. I was going to wrap my arms around her and ask her to forgive me. I was going to introduce her to my daughter.

Helen.

Author's Note

This novel has lived within me for well over a decade. As much as I tried to push it aside over the years, Helen's story persisted in making its way to the page. It would not let me rest until it was told.

My grandmother Helen was a huge presence in my life—from my childhood until I, myself, became a mother. I loved and admired her in all her complexities. I still miss her. After she passed away, I started to write little scenes about her life based on stories she had told me. Of course, looking back now, I deeply regret not asking her more questions when I had the chance—about her time in Boston as a child, what it was like working in Halifax during the war and growing up in a logging camp. Much of what I learned about her life came from my own mother, who knew few details herself. We did, however, know some key things. We knew Helen loved school and adored her father. We knew her mother could be controlling and hard on her.

My mother never knew her own father very well, and we had little information about Edgar's time in the war. I would have liked to know more about all the people in Helen's life, but especially how she persevered through such hardships and heartbreaks. These are the regrets we all have after the people we love are gone.

Over time, the small stories evolved and I knew I was writing a novel. I took some of the circumstances and characters from my grandmother's life, fictionalized them, and wove in scenes from my imagination. (For example, the real Helen had two children by

Edgar, first a son, Bob, in 1937, and then my mother, Colleen.) But ultimately, the story that came from within me, and that I was compelled to tell, is the piece of fiction found in these pages. Although it is not Helen's true-life story, I tried to follow the timeline of her life as closely as possible.

I used the backdrop of the town where she lived most of her life and did my best to realistically portray Truro as it was in the 1930s and '40s. My dear friend and amazing artist, Kim Danio, created the map of Truro using historical and current photographs as reference. This map is meant to be a representation of Truro at the time and many of the buildings are exact renditions as they appeared in the early twentieth century. Some still stand today, including the maternity home, Stanfield's, the bank, the post office, and the court house. I fictionalized many characters from Helen's real family, keeping the same names in many instances, but I also created a cast of characters to help her survive. I gave her a loving confidant in Aunt Gertie, and childhood friends like Madge and the Sullivans in the hopes that perhaps my grandmother had people in her life like them, who supported her and gave her the love she so desperately needed.

During my research for this novel, Tom Stanfield, a longtime family friend, graciously arranged for me to tour the Stanfield's mill and speak with employees. My great-grandmother, grandmother, and mother all worked at Stanfield's at some point in their lives. They each had their own coupon books and sewed in the large, dust-filled rooms with dozens of other ladies. Surprisingly, not much has changed in the mill over the years; hearing the machines whirling and buzzing, looking out the large windows across the marsh, and hearing stories of the generations who have worked there was like stepping back in time. I interviewed two former Stanfield's employees, Bev Young and Calvin Eisner, who worked at the mill for many years. They were a wealth of information, and I fictionalized some of their stories and anecdotes in this novel.

Stanfield's purchased Hewson Woolen Mills in Amherst in the early 1900s and renamed it Amherst Woolen Mills. They manufactured blankets during the First World War. I was unable to establish if Stanfield's still ran this mill during the Second World War, but to help with my storyline I have kept Amherst Woolens running through this timeframe.

I benefitted from the services of the Colchester Historcum in Truro. I particularly appreciated the assistance of archivist Ashley Sutherland. I found information on Stanfield's, logging camps, and the town of Truro during the war—the shops of downtown in particular.

Edgar was a member of the North Nova Scotia Highlanders. Ray Coulson of the Nova Scotia Highlanders Regimental Museum was helpful in confirming facts about my research on the North Novas. I also relied on the book *No Retreating Footsteps: The Story of the North Nova Scotia Highlanders* by Will R. Bird and tried to be true to their timelines and history during the Second World War.

I visited Lunenburg, where Duane Porter, operator of the Halifax & Southwestern Railway Museum, was happy to help me with historical train schedules and knowledge about locomotives during the period of my novel.

My grandmother was a bit of an historian herself, and left behind scrapbooks and envelopes filled with family genealogy records and newspaper clippings. The police officer's account of Helen's father's death was taken directly from the original newspaper clipping, which went into great detail about his death, after being struck by a CNR train.

The real Helen walked from her boarding house on College Road to the Maternity Hospital on Queen Street on July 18, 1946, where she gave birth to my mother. She wore a heavy coat to conceal her large stomach on a sweltering hot day. On July 18, 2020, shortly after Vagrant Press accepted this manuscript to be published, my mother and I went to Truro and found the house on College Road where my grandmother had boarded in 1946. It was a beautiful warm sunny day, and my mother and I walked the same road Helen had seventy-four years earlier, passing many of the same landmarks she did, including Stanfield's. We ended at the former maternity home on Queen Street. It was a marvellous day.

Acknowledgements

The writing process can be an amazing and rewarding journey. It can also be lonely and full of self-doubt. I would not have made it through this crazy roller coaster without the support and encouragement of some truly exceptional people.

First, thank you to my fellow writers.

Many years ago, Donna Morrisey was my mentor through the Humber School of Creative Writing. Donna was the first person to read my words. Her encouraging feedback gave me the confidence I needed to believe in myself and to keep writing. To have the support of someone I have admired for so long has been very humbling indeed. Thank you, Donna.

Chris Benjamin met with me through his role as the Writer in Residence for the South Shore Public Libraries. I am nothing without a deadline, and my discussions with Chris, during the six months preceding COVID, were pivotal to my finally completing this novel. Thank you, Chris.

I met Renée Hartleib through one of her writing workshops. I am grateful for her positive energy and inspiring emails, which helped motivate me to continue writing. Thank you, Renée.

What a pleasant surprise it has been to learn of the extraordinary depth of support and comraderie that exists within the writing community. I am honoured to be welcomed into such a generous group of talented people.

Thank you to Kim Danio for the beautiful map, and for being with me every step of the way. I hope our adventures continue for many years to come!

Thank you to Sylvia Gunnery. My manuscript might still be buried in my drawer if it weren't for your delightfully wise persistence.

My editor, Whitney Moran's enthusiasm and incredibly kind words made me believe this novel was meant to be read by someone other than myself. Thank you, Whitney, for believing in me and for making my publication journey such an exciting and joyful one.

Thank you to Tom Stanfield, Bev Young, Calvin Eisner, Ashley Sutherland, Ray Coulson, and Duane Porter for assisting with my research efforts.

Thank you to the team at Vagrant Press.

A tremendous thank you to my mother, my number-one fan. This has always been for you, Mom.

And finally, thank you to the three amazing men in my life: Beav, Sam, and Finn, xoxo.